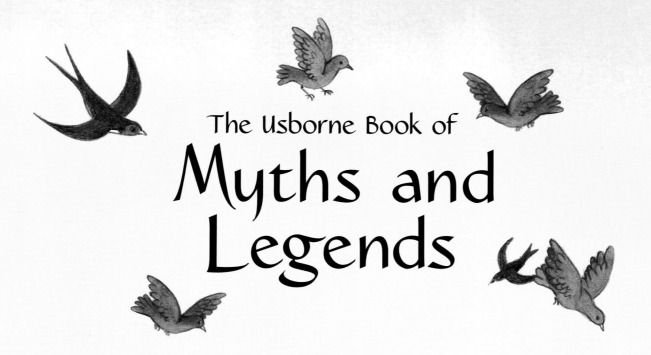

The Usborne Book of
Myths and Legends

Designed by Amanda Gulliver, Nelupa Hussain and Joe Pedley
Cover design by Hanri van Wyk

The Usborne Book of
Myths and Legends

Anna Milbourne, Heather Amery
and Gillian Doherty

Illustrated by Linda Edwards

Contents

Animal fables

Legends of monsters and dragons

A bag full of stories

For thousands of years, all around the world, people have been telling stories. Often, they weren't written down, but told aloud, passed along from person to person. You might come across similar stories from opposite sides of the world. Perhaps they were passed along by storytellers long ago, or maybe people far, far apart just have similar tales to tell. However they travel, stories have a life all of their own, as you'll soon discover.

"Oh please tell me another story. Please," begged Lom, even though his eyelids were heavy with sleep.

"No, it's late. You must go to bed now," said Lom's old servant. Reluctantly, Lom snuggled down, with the story he had just heard still whirling around in his head.

Every night since he was a very small boy, the old servant had told Lom wonderful stories – about powerful gods and goddesses, terrifying dragons and monsters, and all kinds of cunning animals. Lom would hang on to his every word, and wish and wish that each story would never come to an end.

Lom often boasted to his friends about the stories the old servant told him. "You just wouldn't believe how good they are," he'd say.

"Won't you tell them to us?" they asked again and again.

"They sound so exciting."

But Lom refused. "They're *my* stories," he said, "and I won't tell them to anyone."

Sometimes, though, when Lom was by himself, he would whisper the stories into a bag. Now, this might seem like a very strange thing to do, but Lom did like to tell stories; he was just too selfish to share them with his friends.

The years passed by and Lom grew into a handsome young man. Even though he was no longer a child, the old servant still told him stories each night.

Then the time came for Lom to marry. The night before the wedding, the old servant was waiting for Lom in his room when he thought he heard whispering. It seemed to be coming from a bag hanging on the door.

"It's not fair. He's getting married in the morning," muttered a voice. "Think of all the fun he'll be having while we're all squashed in this smelly old bag."

"He should set us free," grumbled another voice. "Surely everybody knows stories need to be told. It's not right to keep us all to himself."

"No, it's not fair to treat us like this," said a third. "We should teach him a lesson."

"What sort of lesson?" came a whole chorus of excited voices from inside the bag.

The old servant's eyes grew wide as he listened. These were the stories he had told Lom. They were talking to one another.

"I've got a plan," said the first story. "It's going to be a hot day tomorrow. I'll turn myself into a well, and when he drinks the water from it, he'll get a terrible pain in his stomach."

"Yes, and I'll turn myself into a watermelon," added the second story. "As soon as he takes a bite, he'll get a terrible pain in his head."

"I'll turn myself into a snake and bite him," said the third story eagerly. "That will give him a terrible pain in his leg too." The bag shook as the stories giggled.

The old servant was horrified. He couldn't believe his stories had become so mean and nasty. All that night, he lay awake, trying to think of a way to stop the stories from spoiling Lom's wedding day.

The next morning, just as Lom was setting off, the old servant rushed out and grabbed his horse's bridle. "Let me lead you," he said to Lom. Panting in the heat, he led the horse up the hill and down the other side, where they came to a well. "I'm thirsty," said Lom. "Let's stop and have a drink."

The old servant pretended he hadn't heard and led the horse on past the well.

8

A little further on, they came to a field full of enormous, juicy watermelons. "They look delicious," said Lom longingly. "Wait a moment while I try one."

But the old man ignored him and kept on going.

As they reached the village where Lom's bride lived, crowds of people came out to greet them. They waved and cheered as Lom passed by.

By the time they reached the bride's house, the old servant was so worried about the snake that he could hardly concentrate on anything. He spent the whole wedding ceremony searching under the seats and peering into corners. "What's wrong with you today?" hissed Lom.

Afterwards, there was a great feast for all the guests, but the old servant hardly touched a thing. Instead, he wandered up and down, reaching into pots and emptying out bowls to check that the snake wasn't there.

"Stop it!" snapped Lom. "You're disturbing everyone. If you can't behave yourself, you'll have to go."

"I'm sorry," muttered the old servant, but he still shuffled around keeping an eye out for the snake.

Eventually, when the last wedding guests had gone happily home, Lom and his bride went to their bed chamber. They were alone at last.

Suddenly, there was a loud knocking on the door, and the old servant burst in, waving a huge stick. "This is the last straw," shouted Lom. "How dare you come bursting in here like this?"

The old servant pushed past him and lifted the rug. There, coiled underneath, was a poisonous snake. With one blow, he killed it and flung it out of the room.

Lom stared at him, open-mouthed. "I don't understand," he said. "How did you know it was there?"

The old servant explained how he'd overheard the stories talking in the bag. "You see, because you didn't pass them on, the stories grew restless and angry, and decided to take their revenge," he said.

Lom could hardly believe what he was hearing. "I had no idea," he said. "Thank you, my old friend. Can you ever forgive me for treating you so badly?"

"Of course," said the old servant, "but you mustn't keep the stories to yourself any more."

"I'm sorry," said Lom. "It was wrong of me. I'll make sure I share them from now on."

So Lom began to tell the stories to his new wife. Each time he did, the bag jiggled about as the stories jostled for their turn. Then, one by one, they hopped out and experienced that moment that every story longs for – to live in the imagination of an eager listener.

Lom's wife loved the stories and couldn't wait to tell them to their children, and, of course, many years later their children told them to *their* children. In fact, the stories are still being told today. I know, because I've heard them. Would you like to hear them too? Then let's begin...

Myths
of
how things came to be

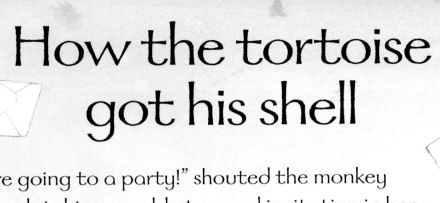

How the tortoise got his shell

"We're going to a party!" shouted the monkey excitedly, clutching a gold-stamped invitation in her paw. "Zeus, the great thunder god, is getting married tomorrow and we're all invited."

Throughout the morning, the skies had been filled with bluebirds, swallows and swifts dropping invitations outside every animal's home. In all the forests and meadows, seas and skies, creatures were squeaking, hopping, singing and chattering with sheer delight.

"Gods throw the very best parties," said the monkey enthusiastically. "Everyone's going to be there."

"Not me," said the tortoise, popping his sleepy head out of his doorway to see what all the fuss was about. "I don't think I can be bothered."

"You can't be bothered!"
exclaimed the monkey in surprise.

"No," yawned the tortoise. "I think
I'd rather just stay at home." He crawled out
of his doorway to warm up in the sun. In those
days, the tortoise didn't have a shell. He was just a bare,
wrinkly animal, who never strayed far from his comfortable
burrow in the ground.

"Well," said the monkey, "you'll be the only one!"

And she was right. The next day, animals from all four
corners of the world trotted and scampered, scurried and flew
to Zeus's summer palace for the party.

And what a party it was! Garlands of flowers and bright
banners hung between the trees, beautiful fountains showered
glittering droplets, and heavenly music wove its way through
the air like gold and silver threads.

Zeus and his bride showed the guests to their places. Laid
out on long tables beneath the trees was the most wonderful
feast, with all kinds of food to suit each and every animal.
There were carrot cakes for the rabbit and seed rolls for the
birds, honey buns for the bear and all the banana splits the
monkey could eat.

As everyone sat down to eat, Zeus suddenly noticed that there was an empty place. "Who's missing?" he asked the squirrel.

"The tortoise," said the squirrel, munching her way through a large nut cluster.

"Where is he?" asked Zeus.

The squirrel shrugged. "He didn't come," she said. "I'm not sure why. Nobody else would have missed this for the world!"

Zeus nodded, looking thoughtful.

After everyone had eaten their fill, the band started to play. Zeus got up with his wife and danced a merry jig and, one by one, the animals left their tables and joined in. They danced in circles and they danced in lines, holding hands together or whirling each other around in pairs.

Night fell and the moon appeared, shining like a huge lantern in the sky. On and on they danced, all through the night. Then the moon slipped away and the waking sun began to stroke her fingers across the sky.

As his tired, happy guests prepared to go home, Zeus gave each of them a gift. He gave a song to the nightingale and a hop to the hare, stripes to the zebra and a pair of humps to the camel. Home the guests went, delighted with their gifts, their ears still ringing with the sound of the music.

14

The next day, Zeus went to visit the tortoise. He found the wrinkly creature sunning himself outside his doorway. "Hello, tortoise," said Zeus. "You weren't at my party last night, so I came to see if you were feeling well."

The tortoise opened one eye and squinted up at Zeus, shading his face against the sun with his front leg. "I'm fine, thank you," he said. "I just didn't feel like coming."

"Really?" said Zeus dangerously. "Why not?"

"There's no place like home," the tortoise replied, shutting his eyes and stretching out in the sunshine.

Zeus, who was famous for his hot temper, erupted in fury. "Well, if you like staying at home *that* much, I'll give you one you can take with you wherever you go," he raged, and he flung out his arms.

KAZOOM! There was a huge clap of thunder and the tortoise was engulfed in a cloud of smoke. Fuming with anger and with his fingertips still smoking, Zeus marched off into the forest.

When the smoke cleared, the tortoise found, to his dismay, that he had a large, hard shell on his back. And since that day, he has had to carry his home with him wherever he goes.

Arachne

All day long, Arachne would sit at her loom weaving the most intricate patterns imaginable. People came from far and wide to admire her work and beg her to make things for them. Arachne loved hearing them say how clever she was and she grew very conceited.

One day, an old woman came to watch. "Athena may be the goddess of weaving, but I'm much more talented," Arachne boasted to her.

"You should be careful what you say," warned the old woman. "Athena will be furious if she hears you."

"I don't care," said Arachne, sticking her chin out proudly. "If she thinks she can do better, she should come here and prove it."

At once, there was a flash of light, and the bent old woman changed into Athena herself. "She *has* come," said the goddess in an icy voice, "and she accepts your challenge. Now, let's see who's the best."

Athena placed her loom beside Arachne's and they began to weave. They worked for hours and hours, hardly even glancing at one another, they were concentrating so hard. News of the competition got around and soon the whole village had gathered there. Everyone watched, spellbound, as the weavings grew and grew.

When at last the two pieces were finished, Athena stared at them in silence. Her own was as impressive as you would expect of a goddess, but Arachne's was something else entirely. Athena had never seen anything so elaborate. Every tiny stitch was as perfect as could be. There was no doubt whose was best.

Athena's face twisted with jealousy. She tore Arachne's weaving from the loom and ripped it to shreds. "Since you're so clever," she snarled, "you shall weave forever, but no one will ever want what you weave."

She touched Arachne on the head and the girl dropped to the ground. Everyone watched in horror as her body shrank to a small, dark blob and her delicate fingers became eight little legs. The tiny, terrified creature scuttled into a dark corner. Arachne had become a spider.

She kept on weaving, making web after beautiful web, only for people to brush them away with their brooms. Her many descendants still make webs today, and if you've ever seen one sparkling in the morning dew, you'll know just how beautiful they are.

Echo and Narcissus

Echo was a pretty wood nymph who loved the sound of her own voice. She talked so much that it was difficult to get a word in when she was around.

One day, the goddess Hera came to the forest where Echo lived, to look for her husband, Zeus. "I know he's here somewhere. Have you seen him?" she asked Echo.

"No, I haven't," said Echo, and Hera started to walk away. "Isn't it a glorious day?" said Echo. But before the goddess could reply, Echo was already chattering about something else. Several times, Hera tried to get away, but each time Echo launched into yet another topic.

By the time Hera finally managed to escape, Zeus was long gone. The goddess was very angry. "You stupid girl. Thanks to your endless prattle, I've missed him," she said irritably. "Since you're so fond of talking, you can always have the last word," she said, "but from now on you will only be able to repeat what other people say to you."

Echo opened her mouth to answer back, but all she could say was, "You."

"You may go now," said Hera.

"Go now," repeated Echo helplessly. Horrified, she clapped her hand to her mouth and stumbled away through the forest.

19

Echo became lonely and miserable. None of her friends wanted to be with her now, for all she ever did was repeat what they said.

Then, one day, she saw Narcissus. Echo had never seen such a handsome young man before and couldn't help falling hopelessly in love. She began to follow him around.

At first, Narcissus took no notice of her; he was very used to girls falling in love with him. But, after a while, he grew irritated. Everywhere he went Echo was there too. "Go away. I don't love you," he said scornfully.

"Love you," answered Echo, still trailing after him.

Narcissus turned on her. "What's wrong with you?" he snapped. "Just leave me alone."

"Alone, alone," came her mournful reply.

Echo knew there was no hope for her love. She grew so sad that she couldn't eat or sleep. Roaming the forest like a restless ghost, she faded a little each day, until eventually she disappeared altogether. Only her voice was left, drifting on the wind, always repeating what anyone said.

The goddess Artemis saw how cruel Narcissus had been and decided to punish him. One afternoon, when he was returning from hunting, Narcissus came across a pool of clear, bright water. As he cupped his hands and dipped them in to drink from it, he caught sight of his reflection. He jerked back in surprise. Then he saw how handsome the face in the water was and he leaned forward and smiled. The face smiled back.

Narcissus had never seen his reflection in a mirror and had no idea that he was looking at himself. "At last I have found a beauty worthy of my love," he thought.

Day after day, he lay staring into the pool, totally entranced. Whenever he spoke, the lips of the face in the water moved too, as if they were trying to talk back to him. When he tried to kiss them, the lips seemed to rise to meet his, but as soon as his own lips touched the water, the surface rippled and the face disappeared.

"Come out," begged Narcissus. "I love you." But his reflection only gazed longingly back at him.

Narcissus couldn't bear it. "I can't live without you," he wept.

Now he felt as Echo had felt and, just as she had done, he pined until he wasted away. In his place, beside the pool, a pretty flower grew. You can still see this flower in spring. It is called a narcissus.

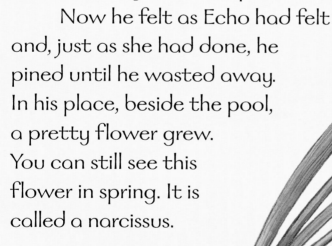

How bees got their stings

"Buzz off!" shouted the queen bee angrily as a big, hairy hand broke into her hive. The hand simply brushed the furious queen and her worker bees aside and scooped out all of their precious, golden honey. The bees buzzed and buzzed in protest, but there was nothing they could do to stop it. You see, in those days, bees were just harmless, fuzzy insects with no way at all of defending themselves.

"We can't go on like this," said the queen bee in despair. "Every time we nearly have a hive full of honey, someone breaks in and steals it all."

The worker bees murmured their agreement.

"Enough is enough," said the queen bee firmly. "Come along, all of you. We're going to see the great god Zeus."

They flew off at once, in the biggest, buzziest swarm anyone had ever seen. They blotted out the sun as they flew overhead, and people stopped to look up in wonder as they passed.

The bees flew up through the fluffy white clouds and high into the sky above. They flew right past the north wind and over a rainbow, and at last they came to Zeus's palace.

"What's all this?" said Zeus when he saw the enormous swarm.

The queen bee bustled up to the god and hovered in the air in front of his nose. "Good afternoon, Zeus," she said, dancing a curtsey. "I have come to see you about a most important matter."

The great god bowed politely to the tiny queen. "In that case," he said, "please come inside and explain."

23

"Very well," said the queen bee, and she flew in through the open door with her entire swarm following behind.

"Do sit down," Zeus said to them. The bees settled all over the polished marble floor, looking for all the world like a large, fuzzy rug. "Your highness," Zeus said to the queen bee, and he laid a red velvet cushion on a throne for her to sit on.

"Thank you," said the queen bee. She settled on the cushion, delicately folded her wings and cleared her throat. "All summer long," she began, "my workers slave away, gathering pollen from countless flowers and making it into honey. But people simply break into our hive whenever they feel like it and steal our honey. We have no way of defending ourselves." The queen quivered with emotion as she spoke. "I'm appealing to you, as one ruler to another, to help us."

Zeus was as fond of honey as anyone, but he didn't like to see the queen bee so upset. He racked his brains to think of a solution. Eventually, he came up with an idea. "I think I can give you a way of defending yourselves," he said. "But it would be a shame if nobody could ever eat honey again. If I give you a weapon that will make people respect you more, will you promise to use it sparingly, and to allow them to take a little honey now and then?"

"Of course," said the queen bee, and her subjects nodded enthusiastically.

"Very well," said Zeus. "Go back to your hives and I'll let you know when the weapon is ready."

24

After the bees had left, Zeus went to his workshop and began to design a weapon so tiny that it could be fitted to the tail of a bee. It was very fiddly work and took him several days. When he had finally finished, he sent a message to the queen bee. She returned, bringing all of her many subjects with her, and Zeus fitted each and every bee with the miniature weapon.

"This weapon," Zeus explained, "causes a painful sting. It will work as many times as you want it to, but you must promise that you'll only use it when it's absolutely necessary."

"We promise," chorused all the little bees. They flew away, wiggling their tails with pleasure, as pleased as punch with their new weapons.

All afternoon, the bees hummed as they worked, gathering nectar and making it into a fresh batch of honey.

The very next morning, just as the queen bee was eating her breakfast, a fat, groping hand pushed its way into the hive and broke off a piece of honeycomb.

"Sting the hand!" shouted the queen bee, and three worker bees dived at the hand and stung it as hard as they could.

"OUCH!" came a yell, and the owner of the hand wrenched it back out of the hive.

"It worked!" exclaimed the queen, and a buzz of excitement went around the hive.

The next day, another hand reached in and tried to scoop out some honey. This time, ten bees zoomed over, their tails ready and quivering. "What are you waiting for?" cried the queen bee. "Sting the hand! Sting the hand!" So all ten bees dived gleefully onto the hand and stung it for all they were worth. Its owner yowled in agony and hauled his hand out of the hive as quickly as he could.

After that, there was no stopping the bees. Giddy with their new power, they stung people for stealing their honey; they stung people for touching their hive; and before long, they even began to sting people for just *looking* at their hive.

Zeus knew nothing of this until one day he asked one of his servants to go and collect some honey to spread on his bread.

The servant turned pale at the mention of honey, but he didn't dare disobey his master. "Right away," he gulped, and hurried off to the hive.

Half an hour later, the servant burst back into the palace. He was in a terrible state. He had red sting marks all over his arms and legs, and on his face too. He flung himself on his knees in front of Zeus and burst into tears.

"What happened to you?" asked Zeus.

"I tried to get you some honey for your bread," wailed the servant. "Honestly I did. But I didn't even get to the hive before all the bees swarmed out and stung me to bits."

"What?" roared Zeus. "I gave them those weapons to protect themselves, not to sting people senseless!"

Zeus stormed straight to the queen bee's hive. As he approached, the bees buzzed out to greet him, but when they saw his thunderous expression, they hurried back inside.

"Come back here this instant!" bellowed Zeus.

The bees peered out fearfully. Then the queen bee flew outside, looking more than a little sheepish.

"You ought to be ashamed of yourselves," raged Zeus, "for being so mean with your honey and so generous with your stings. From now on," he continued, "you may each sting once, and once only. When you do, you will not only lose your ability to sting, but your life as well."

The bees took his words to heart and, from that day to this, they have been more generous with their honey, and a *lot* more careful with their stings.

Pandora's box

"How dare you!" Zeus bellowed at Prometheus. He was furious with him for stealing fire from the gods to give to the people on Earth. "I'll punish you later," he growled. "First, I'm going to teach these people you're so fond of a lesson they won't forget!"

Zeus called the other gods and goddesses before him. "I need you to help me make a special woman," he said, and he told them his plan to punish people.

They set to work at once, shaping a woman from clay. The goddesses showered her with beauty and dressed her in the most exquisite gown. She was absolutely perfect. Then Hermes added the finishing touch, putting curiosity in her heart.

Zeus named the woman Pandora. "Take her to Prometheus's brother, Epimetheus," he ordered Hermes, and took out a box. "Give him this," he said. "He's such a fool that he'll never suspect a thing."

So Hermes flew with Pandora to Epimetheus. "Here is a wife for you," he said. "She is a gift from Zeus."

"Thank you," gasped Epimetheus. He gazed at Pandora, hardly able to believe his good fortune.

"And so is this," said Hermes, handing him the box. "Keep it safe, but do not ever open it."

Soon, Epimetheus and Pandora were married. The two of them lived happily together, and they never exchanged a cross word. The world was a wonderful place to live in then. No one became ill or old and no one was unkind or unpleasant to one another.

But in this perfect world there was one thing that weighed on Pandora's mind — the unopened box. The more she thought about it, the more curious she became. "Let's just have a little peek," she suggested to her husband.

"No. We were told never to open it," said Epimetheus, scared of what would happen. He knew better than to risk making Zeus angry.

Every day, Pandora begged him to open the box, and every day he refused. Then, one morning, when Epimetheus had gone out, Pandora crept into the room where the box was and stared at it. Finally, she made up her mind. She would open it. Hardly daring to breathe, she lifted the lid.

30

A terrible wailing filled the room. She tried to slam the lid down, but it was too late. Out of the box streamed a cloud of hideous winged creatures and with them all kinds of horrible things. There was hate and jealousy, cruelty and anger, hunger and poverty, pain and sickness, old age and death.

One after the other, the creatures flew out of the window. As the last of them disappeared, Epimetheus burst in and saw the open box. "What have you done?" he screamed, so loudly that he almost frightened himself. He and Pandora stared at one another in shocked silence. It was the first time he had ever been angry with her.

Just then, they heard movement inside the box. Fearfully, Pandora peered into it. As she did, something pretty and delicate fluttered out. It was hope. It hovered for a moment in the air, and then flew out of the window.

From that day on, the world would never be the same again. People would suffer all kinds of terrible things, but because they had hope, they would never despair.

31

Maui's land

Long ago, on a small island in a big ocean, a baby boy was born. His mother, Taranga, named him Maui. When she first saw him, her heart grew heavy. Her other four sons were strong and healthy, but this child was small and thin and, at that time, any sickly baby had to be put outside to die.

Taranga loved her baby son, and was desperate to find a way to save him. One dark night, she took Maui and hurried down to the seashore. There she found a piece of bone. She scratched Maui's name on it and hung it around his neck. Then she made a cradle of floating seaweed. She kissed Maui and laid him inside. "May the gods look after you," she whispered as she pushed it out onto the dark sea.

The cradle drifted away, with Maui sleeping soundly inside it. As it bobbed along, some dolphins saw it and came to see what it was. Gently, they nudged the cradle with their noses. Then the waves took hold of it and carried it along the coast, far away from where its journey had begun.

Morning came, and the sun's golden rays spilled across the sea. Tama, a wise old fisherman, was just setting out in his boat when he caught sight of something lying on the sand. "What can this be?" he thought to himself, and went over to see. The very last thing he expected to find was a sleeping baby. He looked around in surprise, but the seashore was deserted.

Tama bent down and read the name on the piece of bone. "Maui," he said softly, "I feel in my heart that you are a very special boy." He picked up the sleeping baby and carried him home, where he fed him and looked after him.

In time, Maui grew from a thin, weak baby into a fine young man. Tama taught him everything he could. He taught him how to fish and hunt, how to understand the language of birds and animals, and even how to understand what other people were thinking. "Soon it will be time for you to go home," said Tama one morning.

"Don't be silly," laughed Maui. "This is my home."

"This will always be your home," said Tama, "but you have another home too..." and he told him the story of how he was washed up by the sea.

As the weeks went by, Maui began to wonder about his family. Sometimes, he would wander off into the forest to be alone with his thoughts. One day, he lost track of time and strayed much further than he had ever been before.

It was just beginning to grow dark when Maui came across a house. He could hear snatches of conversation coming from inside, so he crept up to the door and saw a woman and her four sons eating their evening meal. "Who's there?" said one of the young men suddenly.

Maui stepped out of the shadows. "It's me, Maui," he said. The four young men sprang to their feet, ready to defend themselves against the stranger.

"Wait," said their mother, stepping forward to look at Maui. As soon as she saw the piece of bone around his neck, she knew this was her son. She threw her arms around him, laughing with joy. "The gods have sent you back to me," she cried. She turned to her other four sons. "This is your lost brother," she said. "Aren't you going to welcome him?"

But Maui's brothers weren't so pleased to see him, and as the days went by they grew more and more jealous. "Our mother loves that brat more than us," muttered the eldest. "Let's find a way to turn her against him."

Secretly whispering together, they made a plan to go fishing very early the next morning, and then tell their mother that Maui had been too lazy to go with them.

Thanks to Tama's teaching, Maui knew what they were thinking and made his own plan. Before dawn, he hurried down to the seashore and hid in his brothers' fishing canoe, covering himself with nets.

A little while later, Maui's brothers arrived. They were so busy chatting that they didn't notice him and began to paddle out to sea. When they were a long way from shore, one of them began to chuckle. "Mother should be waking up now," he said, "and she'll find lazybones Maui fast asleep."

"I'm not lazy," said Maui indignantly, and he threw off the nets and sat up.

His brothers were furious to see him there, but it was too late to do anything about it, so instead they began to fish.

34

They fished for hours and hours, but caught nothing at all. "Why don't we paddle further out to sea?" said Maui. "There are plenty more fish there."

The brothers scowled and muttered, but they did as Maui suggested. "Since you're so clever, let's see you catch some fish," said one of them irritably.

Maui smiled to himself. He took out a fish hook he had made, tied it to a long line, and dropped it over the side of the canoe. For a while, nothing happened. "Why, you're no better at catching fish than we are," jeered his brothers.

At just that moment, there was a sharp tug on the line. "Quick! Help me pull it in," shouted Maui.

Together, the five brothers heaved on the line. It was so heavy that the canoe dipped dangerously, almost tipping them into the sea. They pulled and pulled for all they were worth. At last, they saw something rising slowly in the water. "It must be a giant fish," shouted one brother.

Another peered over the side of the canoe. "No, it's not," he cried excitedly. "It's an island. Maui has fished up an island." And he was right. A beautiful, green island, shaped almost like a fish, surged up out of the sea.

Maui and his four brothers waited for it to settle and jumped ashore. "This part is mine," said the eldest. "I should have the biggest piece."

"No, it's mine," said the second brother. "I was here first." They began to fight. They kicked and punched, and as they rolled around the island they bashed against it, throwing up mountains and gouging out valleys. Suddenly, there was a crack like thunder, and the island split in two.

Maui's brothers stared at one another fearfully. "Let's get out of here," said the eldest. The others needed no persuasion. They jumped into their canoe, and paddled all the way home.

Maui watched them go, without any feeling of sadness. He had made a new land and he didn't mind being alone there.

One day, other people would live in Maui's land too. It became known as New Zealand. If you look at a map and imagine how the islands would look joined together, you can see that it really does look a little like a fish.

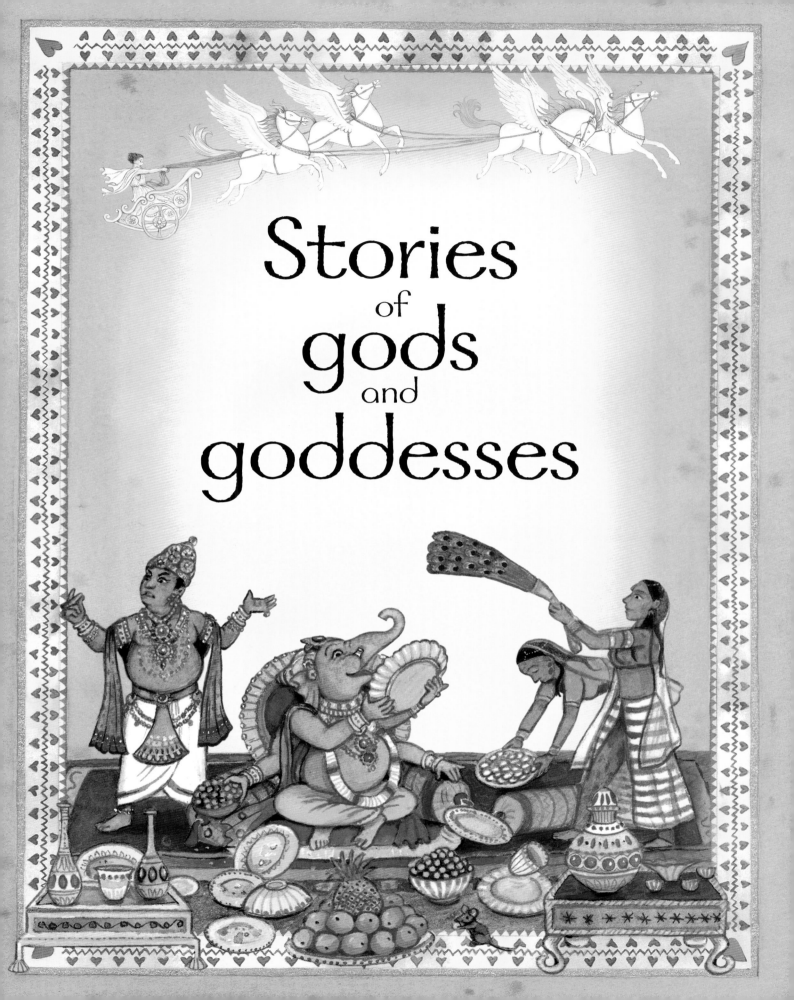

Stories
of
gods
and
goddesses

The biggest banquet

Kubera was the richest person in the world. He was also a terrible show-off. He threw lavish parties and built huge temples and extravagant palaces, just so people could see how rich and generous he was. But no matter how much money he spent, he just seemed to get richer and richer.

One day, Kubera decided to hold the biggest banquet the world had ever seen. Anyone who was anyone would be there — the wisest scholars and the richest businessmen, the most important noblemen and the most powerful kings and queens. But that wasn't all. As his special guests, Kubera was going to invite the god Shiva and his wife, the goddess Parvati.

"Everybody's going to be so impressed," he thought, rubbing his chubby hands together. "I'm so fabulously wealthy that even the gods come to my palace to eat their fill."

Before long, all of Kubera's servants were bustling around his palace preparing for the great feast. They wrote invitations on perfumed paper and sent them all over the world; they bought jewel-encrusted goblets, gold and silver serving dishes, silken cushions and richly embroidered rugs; and then they began to prepare thousands upon thousands of dishes of mouth-watering food.

Meanwhile, Kubera went to visit the god Shiva. "Lord Shiva," he said, bowing down, "I am holding the biggest, most

38

spectacular banquet there has ever been, and I would like you and Parvati to be my special guests."

Knowing what a show-off Kubera was, Shiva answered with a smile, "I'm sorry, Kubera, but we can't come. We have too much to do here."

"But you can't say no!" blurted Kubera. "I've already told everyone that you're coming."

Shiva raised his eyebrows. It was a risky thing to tell a god what he could and could not do.

After thinking for a moment, Shiva said, "My Ganesha enjoys a good banquet. He could come instead." Ganesha was Shiva's son — a short, fat boy with an elephant's head. He was a mischievous little god who absolutely adored his food.

"Thank you," said Kubera gratefully, and he hurried home.

The day of the banquet came and the palace looked magnificent. Servants scurried around scattering rose petals across the marble floors as Kubera waited
eagerly for his guests.

When Ganesha
arrived, Kubera led him to a
special golden throne. "I'm hungry," said
the little elephant god as soon as he sat down.
Kubera clicked his fingers and hundreds of
servants appeared, carrying dishes piled high with the
most exquisite food imaginable.

Ganesha began to eat immediately. He gobbled up
the food without stopping once and, in just a few minutes,
every single dish in front of him was empty.

"I'm still hungry," Ganesha grumbled.

Kubera's servants rushed to bring him more food, but
Ganesha only ate faster and faster. Soon, he was licking
dishes clean almost before they were laid down. In no time
at all, he had devoured the entire banquet.

Kubera looked worried. He waved his hands at the servants, who hurried away to cook more food.

"I'm hungry," wailed Ganesha. He stormed into the kitchen and started to eat the food they were cooking. When that was all gone, he broke down the doors to the storerooms and gulped down everything he could find there. He ate and ate and ate. Soon, there wasn't a scrap of food left anywhere in Kubera's palace.

"I'm still hungry!" Ganesha trumpeted. He stomped back into the banquet hall and began eating the gold and silver dishes, chewing them up as if they were sweets. Then, to Kubera's horror, Ganesha picked up the throne he'd been sitting on and swallowed it whole.

Next, he burst into Kubera's treasury and ate up all of his money and precious jewels. "I want more!" Ganesha shouted, waving his fists and stamping his feet. But by now there really was nothing left for him to eat.

"If there isn't anything else," Ganesha said, "I might just have to eat..." – he swung around to look at Kubera – "YOU!"

A look of horror spread across Kubera's face. He turned and fled, and the little elephant god chased after him. They ran through the palace and into the gardens, across the city and over the hills. "Come back," panted Ganesha. "I'm hungry!"

Kubera ran and ran until his legs felt like lead. As he stumbled breathlessly around a corner, he tripped and fell. He found himself at the feet of Lord Shiva.

"What's all this?" asked Shiva.

Before Kubera could reply, Ganesha ran up to them. "He doesn't have anything else for me to eat," he wailed, "but I'm still hungry!"

"Go and ask your mother for something," said Shiva, and, to Kubera's relief, Ganesha turned and headed for home.

Shiva helped Kubera to his feet. "So how did your banquet go?" he asked gently. "Was it impressive?"

Kubera was ashamed. "Not really," he mumbled.

"But I thought you were so wealthy and generous that even the gods eat their fill at your palace," chuckled Shiva.

Kubera blushed bright red. "I'm sorry for being such a show-off," he said quietly. Then he stopped and his mouth dropped open. Ganesha was coming back. Without another word to Shiva, Kubera sped off down the hillside.

Ganesha giggled. "You don't have to run away any more," he called. "I'm full now!"

The chariot of the sun

Every morning, the god Helios began his journey across the sky. Driving the chariot of the sun, he spread golden light and warmth all over the world.

One afternoon, a group of boys was watching from the ground as the sun god's chariot raced for the horizon. "That's my father," said one boy proudly.

"Don't be silly, Phaethon," laughed his friends.

"It *is*," insisted Phaethon angrily, but his friends only teased him all the more. Their taunts hurt his feelings, for he had never actually met his father.

"I'll show you," he muttered and stormed off to find his mother. "Everyone's laughing at me," he complained. "They won't believe the sun god is my father. How can I prove it?"

"Perhaps you should speak to your father about it," suggested his mother, and she told Phaethon where to find him.

There was no mistaking the palace of the sun god, for it was almost as dazzling as the sun itself. The walls were made of shining gold, and columns embedded with gems of every kind held up a roof of polished ivory. Phaethon walked slowly up the glittering steps. At the top, he paused for a moment, and then timidly he pushed open the heavy doors.

He found himself in a great hall, more splendid than anything he'd ever seen. There before him was his father, a fiery presence in a shimmering silken robe, seated on a throne covered with rubies. His face shone with warmth. "Welcome, my son," said Helios. "What brings you here?"

Shielding his eyes from the great god's brilliance, Phaethon gave a low bow. "Father," he said quietly, "I've come to ask you to grant me a wish."

His father beamed. "Anything you like," he said. "Just name it and I promise it will be yours."

"You're so important and powerful that no one will believe that you're my father," explained Phaethon. "Would you let me drive your chariot, just for one day?" he asked eagerly. "If my friends saw me, they'd know it's true."

His father's face fell. "That's impossible. It's much too dangerous," he said, shaking his head. "How can a mere boy control the chariot of the sun?"

"But you promised," blurted Phaethon.

"Yes, I did," said his father, with a troubled heart. "If I could take it back, I would, but I will not break my word."

He gave his son a powerful medicine so that he wouldn't be burned. Then he took off his crown of rays and placed it upon Phaethon's head. "Follow me," he said.

Phaethon's face glowed as his father led him out to the golden chariot. It was as if he was in a dream. He watched in wonder as the sun god's three daughters harnessed the team of magnificent winged horses. The horses snorted impatiently and danced from side to side, eager to begin their journey.

45

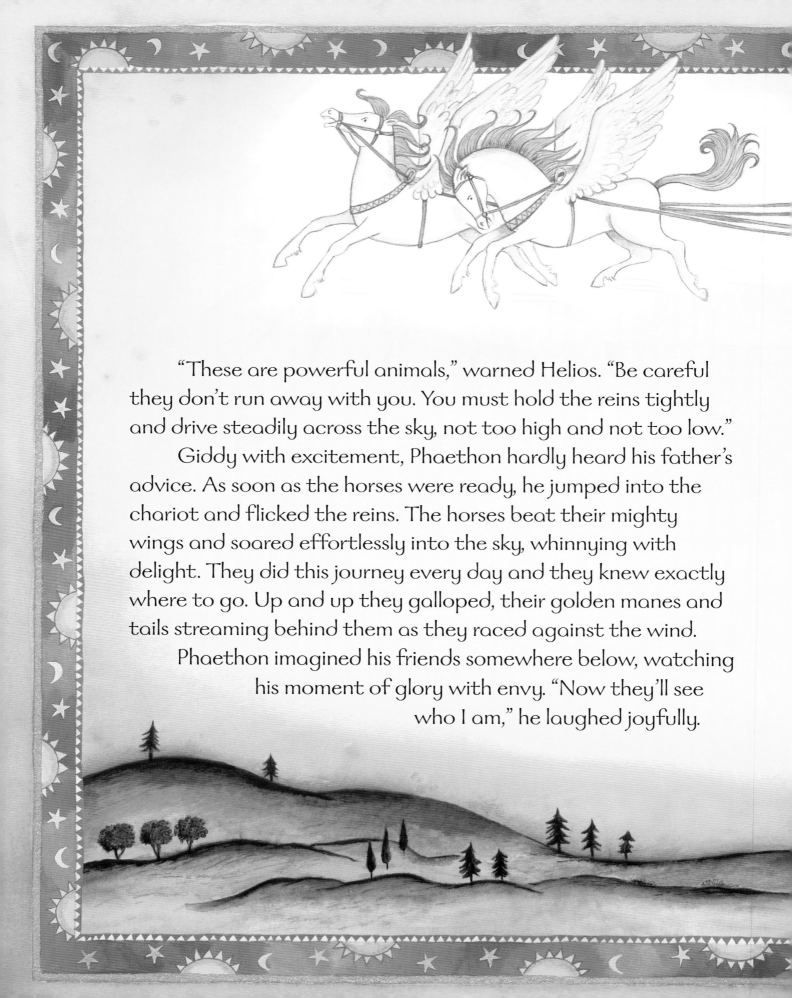

"These are powerful animals," warned Helios. "Be careful they don't run away with you. You must hold the reins tightly and drive steadily across the sky, not too high and not too low."

Giddy with excitement, Phaethon hardly heard his father's advice. As soon as the horses were ready, he jumped into the chariot and flicked the reins. The horses beat their mighty wings and soared effortlessly into the sky, whinnying with delight. They did this journey every day and they knew exactly where to go. Up and up they galloped, their golden manes and tails streaming behind them as they raced against the wind.

Phaethon imagined his friends somewhere below, watching his moment of glory with envy. "Now they'll see who I am," he laughed joyfully.

After a while, Phaethon glanced
down. He could no longer see his father.
"If I can't see my father," he reasoned, "then
my father won't be able to see me, and nor will my friends."
Suddenly, he felt dizzy. It seemed a very, very long way down.
Hardly able to focus, he loosened the reins.

The horses immediately felt them go slack. They
stretched out their necks, but felt no response. With no one
to control them, they bolted from their usual path.

The chariot lurched from side to side, tossed like a ship
on a stormy sea. The horses climbed higher and higher, above
the clouds and into the vast, unknown universe beyond.
"Stop!" cried Phaethon, pulling on the reins. "I'll never find
my way home." But the horses didn't even slow down.

Up among the stars, Phaethon found not the bright cities of the gods that he had imagined, but terrifying monsters that loomed from the darkness, threatening to snatch him. Wild with fright, he dropped the reins.

Suddenly, the chariot began to hurtle downwards. As it blazed through the heavens, it burned brighter and brighter, leaving behind a great scar of stars. Soon, it came so close to the mountains that it scorched their peaks. As it went lower still, its heat made the rivers and oceans boil. Fire swept across the land, setting forests ablaze and reducing great cities to ashes.

"My foolish son," wept Helios when he saw what was happening. "I knew it was too dangerous. If only I hadn't promised..."

Zeus saw all of this too, from his palace on Mount Olympus. "If I don't stop him, that foolish young man will destroy the whole world," he roared angrily, and he picked up a thunderbolt and hurled it at the chariot.

As the thunderbolt struck, the horses tore free, but the chariot split into pieces. Phaethon tumbled through the sky like a shooting star and plunged into a river below.

The daughters of the sun god came down to the river and wept for their brother. For days, weeks, months, they stayed there. Eventually, they became rooted to the ground, and little by little they turned into weeping willows, trailing their branches sorrowfully in the river.

Indra's curse

Once there was a man called Thintha. He had a wife called Kalavati, who everybody said was the most beautiful woman on Earth. But, as Thintha knew, Kalavati was no ordinary woman; she was an apsaras, a magical being whose job it was to sing for the god Indra.

Every morning, Kalavati flew up to heaven, and every evening, she came home to her husband. They lived very happily like this for a long time.

One day, Kalavati said, "I'll be coming home late this evening. Indra has invited some of the other gods to a special celebration. He's asked all the apsarases to sing."

Thintha was suddenly seized with curiosity. "Take me with you," he begged. "I'd love to see what heaven is like."

Kalavati shook her head. "It's forbidden for humans to go there. If Indra found out..." She shuddered at the very thought.

"Just this once," coaxed Thintha. "I won't tell a soul." He pleaded and pleaded with her until, at last, Kalavati agreed to take him. Using her magic, she shrank Thintha to the size of a caterpillar and hid him inside a lotus flower. Then she tucked the flower in her hair and went to Indra's celebration.

49

From his hiding place, Thintha
saw a world no human being had ever
even dreamed of. He watched gods float on
soft clouds; he listened to enchanted music; and
he heard the magical song of the apsarases, their
voices more delicate than a hundred crystal bells. Indra
even had a jester who, near the end of the evening, turned
himself into a goat and did a comical dance. It was the funniest
thing Thintha had ever seen. He laughed helplessly, clamping his
hands over his mouth so that
no one would hear him.

When the party was over, Kalavati took
Thintha home and turned him back to his normal size.
She was very relieved that they hadn't been caught.

The couple went back to their normal lives. The next day,
Kalavati went to heaven as usual and Thintha stayed behind.
His head was spinning with everything he'd seen, so he decided
to go for a walk. He wandered around the
market square, his mind full of gods
and clouds and music.

Suddenly, Thintha spotted a goatherd leading a goat that looked exactly like the one he'd seen the night before. He rushed up to it and shouted, "Dance!"

"Goats don't dance," scoffed the goatherd.

"This one does," insisted Thintha. "Go on then," he urged the goat. "I know you can. I saw you dance for Indra in heaven last night."

But the goat only stared at him with its yellow eyes.

"Go home and rest," laughed the goatherd. "The sun must have fried your brain."

Word spread around the city, and soon everyone was laughing about the madman asking the goat to dance. Before long, Indra got to hear of it. The god realized what must have happened and was absolutely furious.

He summoned Kalavati to him. "How dare you bring a human being into heaven," he thundered.

"I'm sorry," said Kalavati, trembling with fear. "It will never happen again."

"No, it won't," raged Indra. "I'll make sure of that. Say goodbye to your husband. At midnight tonight, you will be turned to stone. You will stand as a marble pillar in the temple. Only when the temple is knocked down will you be released."

Kalavati fled, sobbing, to Thintha and told him about the curse. He hugged her and tried to comfort her, but he knew there was nothing else he could do. Eventually, they both fell into an exhausted sleep.

52

When Thintha woke up the next morning, Kalavati was gone. He ran to the temple. There, in place of one of the pillars, was his beloved Kalavati, turned to stone. "I'm so sorry," wept Thintha. "It's all my fault. I'll find a way to set you free, I promise."

He leaned against the pillar and tried to think. The king would never agree to knock down the temple without a good reason. But nobody was ever going to believe that Thintha's wife had been turned to stone.

All day long, Thintha racked his brains. Then, just as the light of the setting sun began to spill through the temple door, an idea came to him.

He raced home, found four little pots and filled them with Kalavati's necklaces, bangles and other jewels. When night came, and the whole city was sleeping soundly, he crept into the deserted streets and buried them around the city.

Early the next morning, the first few people to emerge saw Thintha, disguised as a holy man, wandering about muttering. Word spread that a holy man had come to the city. The more Thintha wandered and muttered, the more people thought that he must be very holy indeed.

53

The king soon got to hear about the holy man and came to the market square to meet him.

Just as the king approached, a crow happened to fly overhead, cawing loudly. Thintha looked up and laughed. "Thank you, my friend," he called.

"You know how to speak to animals!" exclaimed the king. "Tell me. What did it say?"

"It told me that there is treasure buried beneath my feet," said Thintha. "You may have it, if you like. I've no need of it."

The king pointed at the ground. "Dig," he ordered one of his servants.

The servant dug a hole and uncovered one of the pots of jewels. He handed the pot to the amazed king.

The king and Thintha strolled around the city together talking. Soon, they found themselves in the middle of a park, where Thintha stopped. A moment later, a jackal called in the distance. Thintha smiled. "Thank you," he called back.

"What did it say?" the king asked eagerly.

"There is treasure buried underneath my feet," said Thintha. The king's servant dug again, and again he found a pot of jewels.

They walked on together. To the king's astonishment, they uncovered another pot of jewels near the palace and a fourth right in front of the temple. The king turned to Thintha. "I've never met anyone with such incredible powers," he said. "Come into the temple and let's pray together."

54

Inside the temple, Thintha stopped beside the pillar where poor Kalavati was trapped in stone. Tears filled her stone eyes and began to run down her cheeks.

"What's this?" asked the king, astounded.

Thintha, whose eyes had also filled with tears, turned to the king and said, "She's weeping because you are going to die very soon."

"Die?" gasped the king. "Me?"

"Yes," nodded Thintha gravely. "You will die in three days' time if this temple is still standing."

After everything the king had seen, he believed him. "Guards!" he shouted. "Knock this temple down. I want it gone by tomorrow."

That very evening, the temple was brought tumbling to the ground. Thintha watched anxiously and, as the last pillars fell, he saw a figure, just visible through the dust.

"Kalavati?" he whispered. The figure came closer. It was she. They fell into each others' arms, laughing for joy.

When Indra heard how Thintha had rescued Kalavati, he roared with laughter. He showered blessings on the happy couple and made sure they were never parted again.

Thor's hammer

"Where's my hammer?" roared Thor, making the mountains tremble with the power of his voice. The other gods stopped what they were doing and looked around nervously. They knew there would be no peace until the hammer was found.

Thor was the god of thunder. He was a great giant of a god, with wild, red hair, and his magic hammer was his most treasured possession. When he threw it into the air, lightning flashed and thunder rolled. Without it, he was completely lost.

"It was right here," he muttered, scrabbling around beside his bed. "I'm sure it was. That's where I always leave it." But on this morning the hammer wasn't there.

Thor stormed around, searching everywhere for his hammer. His great, shaggy beard bristled with his anger and his face was like thunder. "Who's stolen my hammer?" he yelled at everyone he met.

56

When he ran into Loki, he
bellowed, "If you've taken it, I'll..."
"Of course I haven't," said Loki.
He was always playing pranks on the
other gods, but he knew better
than to take Thor's hammer.

"I bet Thrym's stolen it," Loki added quickly,
as Thor glared at him. "Why don't I help you find it?"
Without waiting for an answer, Loki hurried to see
the goddess Freya. "I'm helping Thor to look for his hammer,"
he explained. "Can I borrow your feather cloak?"
"Of course," said Freya, handing it to him.
As soon as Loki put it on, the feathers shivered and the
magic cloak carried him high into the air. He spread out the
cloak and flew swiftly to Jotunheim, the land of the giants.
There, wandering among the snow-covered
mountains, he found Thrym, the king of the frost giants.
"What are you doing here?" boomed Thrym.
"I'm looking for Thor's hammer. Have you seen it?"
asked Loki.

"I stole it," growled Thrym, "and I've hidden it so deep inside the Earth that no one will ever find it."

"But Thor needs it more than a mighty giant like you," said Loki. "Haven't you heard the fuss he's making?"

Thrym thought for a while. "All right. If Freya will come here and marry me, I'll give the hammer to her," he said at last.

"I'll have to see what Freya thinks," said Loki, with a frown. He flew back to Thor and together they went to see her.

"What?" shrieked Freya. "Marry that ugly oaf? Is he crazy?"

"Oh, please," begged Thor.

"No," she screamed. "Absolutely no way."

By this time, the other gods had all gathered around to see what the noise was about. When they heard about Thrym's offer, they were delighted. They knew how grumpy Thor would be until he got his hammer back, so they too tried to persuade Freya to marry Thrym.

But Freya wasn't having any of it.

Then Heimdall stepped forward. "I've got an idea," he said.

Freya glared at him. "Go on," she said suspiciously.

"We could dress Thor up as Thrym's bride," he suggested. "If we cover his face with a veil, Thrym will think he's Freya. That way, Thor will get his hammer back and Freya doesn't have to marry Thrym."

Now it was Thor's turn to object. "No way! You expect me, the mighty Thor, to dress up as a girl?" he yelled. "I've never heard such a stupid idea. I won't do it."

"Oh, I see. It's all right for me to marry that great lump, but you won't even wear a dress," said Freya indignantly. "It is *your* hammer, remember?"

Eventually, the other gods persuaded Thor to give it a try. They dressed him up in a beautiful white dress, hung jewels around his neck and covered his face and shaggy mane of hair with a veil. "A bride fit for a giant," giggled Freya.

Meanwhile, Loki sent word to Thrym that Freya would marry him. Then he dressed up as Thor's maid and, with Thor grumbling loudly, the two set off for Jotunheim.

All the giants had gathered for this special occasion and an enormous wedding feast was laid out in the banquet hall. With great ceremony, Thrym led Thor to the head of the table, and sat down beside him. "What would you like to eat, my dear?" he asked politely. "Perhaps a little slice of roasted ox?"

Thor gave a disapproving grunt. He was hungry. Keeping his face hidden beneath the veil, he swallowed eight whole salmon, gobbled down an entire roasted ox and tipped a whole tray of sweets down his throat.

The giants watched in astonishment. Thrym's new bride ate even more than they did. "What a splendid appetite you have, my dear," said Thrym, though secretly he was thinking what a lot she would cost to feed.

Seeing Thrym's startled look, Loki stepped in. "Freya's been so excited about the wedding, she hasn't eaten for days," he whispered in his ear.

Thrym gave a great beam of pleasure, and turned to his bride. He lifted the corner of the veil to kiss her, but when he saw Thor's fierce, bloodshot eyes glaring back at him, he jumped back in horror.

"Poor Freya is exhausted," said Loki quickly. "She hasn't been able to sleep for thinking about you."

Thrym cheered up again. He could hardly believe that his bride was so eager to marry him.

When the feast was over, Thor's hammer was brought in. "Here you are, my dear," said Thrym, placing it in his bride's lap.

Immediately, Thor jumped up and tore off his veil. "I'm Thor and this is *my* hammer," he roared, swinging it around his head.

Thrym and the other giants stared at him in total disbelief. It was the strangest thing they had ever seen. Thor seized his chance. Before they could gather their wits, he hitched up his dress and fought his way out of the hall, wielding his precious hammer.

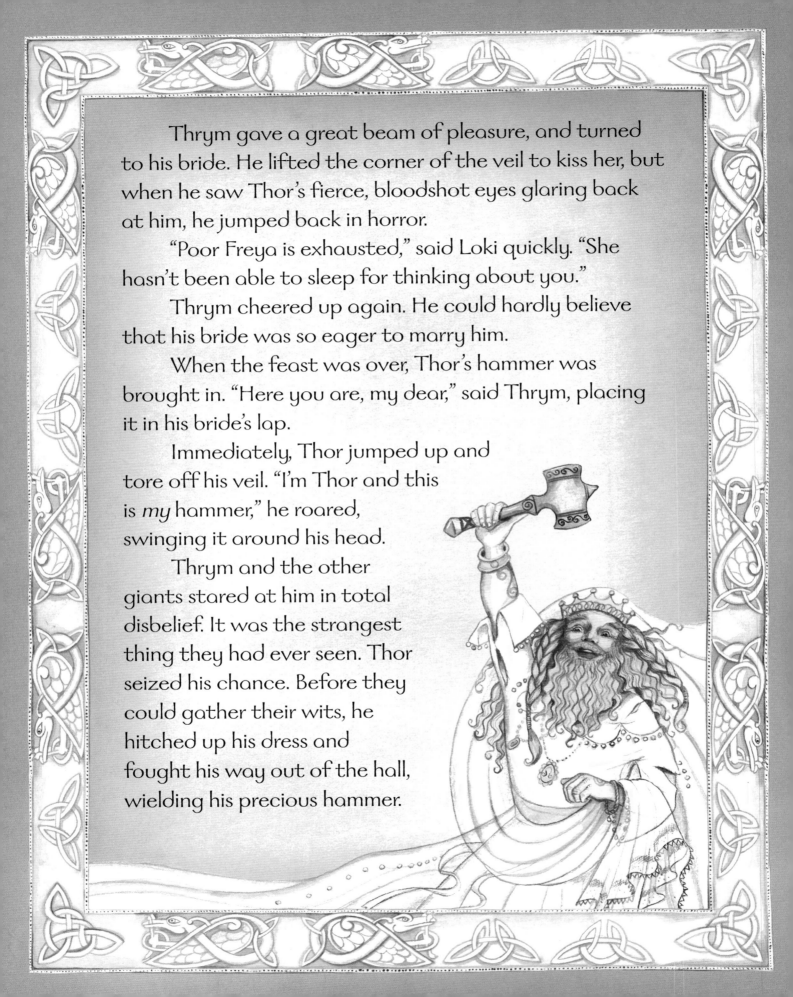

The wicked wish

Bhasmasura was very, very wicked. He wished for nothing more than to make everyone – even the gods – afraid of him.

One day, Bhasmasura heard a story about a holy man who had prayed for so long that the god Shiva had appeared to him and granted him a wish. Bhasmasura thought this might be a good way to have his own wish granted, and so he sat down on the top of a mountain and began to pray to Shiva. For years and years, he prayed non-stop. He sat there so long that moss grew on his shoulders and birds began to nest in his hair.

Shiva was so impressed with Bhasmasura's dedication that he came to visit him. "You have done well to pray for so long," he said. "What can I do for you?"

"Nothing, my Lord," said Bhasmasura, with a cunning glint in his eye. "Just your blessing is enough for me."

This answer impressed Shiva even more. "There must be something I could give you," the god said. "Wish for anything you like and it shall be granted."

"Did you say *anything*?" Bhasmasura said, grinning wickedly. "Well, in that case, I wish that anybody whose head I touch with my right hand will be transformed into a heap of ashes."

Shiva looked worried. This wasn't the kind of wish a good person would make, but he had said that he would grant Bhasmasura anything and so he had to keep his word. "Granted," he said reluctantly.

"Allow me to test out my new power before you go," Bhasmasura said, laughing nastily, and he stretched out his hand. Shiva ducked out of the way just in time, and Bhasmasura snatched the air. Suddenly, Shiva realized the danger he was in. With Bhasmasura close behind him, the mighty god fled. He raced over hills and tore through valleys, leaped over streams and scrambled through forests.

"How am I going to get out of this?" thought Shiva, as he stumbled towards a steep mountain.

"You look as if you could use some help," said an amused voice. Perched on a rock high above Shiva's head sat the god Vishnu.

"Am I glad to see you!" Shiva gasped, trying to catch his breath.

"Hide here for a moment," said Vishnu. "Let me see what I can do."

Seconds later, when Bhasmasura came charging up the mountain, he found a woman standing in his path. "Which way did Shiva go?" he demanded roughly. But when he saw the woman's face, he came to an abrupt stop — she was utterly enchanting.

"Why don't you rest here for a while?" said the woman gently. "You look tired."

Bhasmasura was bewitched. "What's your name?" he asked. "I must have you as my wife."

The woman laughed, a soft, musical laugh. "My name is Mohini," she said, "but I cannot be your wife."

"Why not?" growled Bhasmasura.

"I couldn't possibly marry anyone who doesn't dance as well as I do," said Mohini.

"I can dance just as well as you," leered Bhasmasura. "I'll show you. Any dance you do, I can copy."

Mohini glanced at his big, awkward body and a smile appeared on her lips. "All right then," she said. "Can you do this?" She stepped away from Bhasmasura and danced a few steps, as light as a feather on her feet.

Bhasmasura watched and then danced the same steps, his big feet scuffing up the dust.

Mohini nodded. "But can you do this?" she said, twirling away from him. Round and round she danced, as gracefully as a swallow on a breeze.

Bhasmasura copied, flinging himself around like an overweight buffalo.

"Not bad," said Mohini. "But watch this. If you can copy me this time, then I'll marry you." She danced on, moving so quickly that her feet were a blur. Then, turning to Bhasmasura, she placed her fingertips delicately on the top of her head and sank slowly to the ground.

"Yes, yes," grunted Bhasmasura impatiently. "I can do that." The ground shook beneath his thumping feet as he leaped and twirled with all his might. Then, turning to Mohini, he placed his right hand on top of his head and grinned. "You're mine, all m—"

But before he could finish his sentence, he had turned himself into a heap of ashes.

As Shiva stepped out from his hiding place behind a boulder, Mohini gave one last tinkling laugh and vanished. In her place appeared Vishnu, still smiling.

"Thank you, Vishnu," said Shiva gratefully. "I thought I'd never escape."

"Any time," Vishnu replied. And with that, the two gods set off together down the mountain, leaving the ashes to scatter gently in the wind.

Cupid and Psyche

"My youngest daughter is the most beautiful girl in the world," boasted Psyche's father.

"Of course she is," agreed his wife. "Why, she's even more beautiful than Venus."

Venus, the goddess of love, overheard them. "What nonsense!" she raged. "How could an ordinary girl be more beautiful than a goddess?"

Fuming with jealousy, she stormed off in search of her son, Cupid. She found him lazing by the river with his bow and arrows beside him. Of course, these were no ordinary arrows. Anyone struck by one would fall head over heels in love with the very next person they saw.

Venus told Cupid what had happened. "You must help me teach them a lesson," she said. "I want you to make that wretched girl fall in love with the most miserable and hideous creature alive. Then we'll see what use her so-called beauty is."

"What fun!" chuckled Cupid, rubbing his hands together in glee. There was nothing he enjoyed more than causing mischief, so he flew away at once to look for Psyche.

He found her asleep on a grassy hill. With an impish grin, he took an arrow from his quiver and carefully drew back his bow string. But, just as he fired, he tripped. Instead of flying into Psyche's heart, the arrow pierced his leg.

Cupid gazed at Psyche and a dreamy look came over his face. He fell in love with her right there and then. "What should I do?" he thought. "If my mother finds out, she'll be furious." Somehow, he had to keep it a secret. Gently, he picked up the sleeping Psyche and carried her away.

When Psyche opened her eyes, she gazed around in awe, thinking she was still dreaming. She was in a beautiful palace, surrounded by all kinds of treasures. At that moment, the door opened and huge silver platters laden with all kinds of delicious-looking food floated before her, as if carried by the wind. In the corner, the strings of a golden harp moved all by themselves and music filled the room.

"Don't be afraid," said the voice of Cupid. "You'll be happy here with me, as long as you never try to find out who I am. If you do, I must leave forever."

The next night, and for many nights afterwards, Cupid came to the palace when it was dark and stayed with Psyche. He left before it grew light, so she never saw him. At first, she was frightened, but he was so gentle and spoke so sweetly that she soon began to look forward to his visits.

But Psyche missed her family and longed to see her sisters. "Please," she begged Cupid, "can't they come to visit?"

Cupid didn't think it was a good idea, but he couldn't bear to see Psyche unhappy, so eventually he agreed.

The next day, Psyche had her sisters brought to the palace. They were were extremely envious. "Who *is* this mysterious man of yours?" they asked. "He must be very rich."

When Psyche couldn't give them a proper answer, her sisters began to tease her, and she had to admit that she had never actually seen him.

"He must be a monster," they sneered spitefully. "Why else wouldn't he show himself to you?"

"Go away. I won't listen to you," said Psyche, putting her hands over her ears.

When her sisters had gone, Psyche became more and more curious. That night, as Cupid was sleeping, she crept downstairs and lit an oil lamp. Then she tiptoed back and held it up to his face. She was overjoyed to discover that he was not monstrous at all, but young and handsome. Eagerly, she bent down to kiss him and, as she did, a drop of hot oil fell from the lamp onto his arm.

"Ouch!" cried Cupid, waking up immediately. When he saw Psyche, he shook his head. "I told you not to try to find out who I am," he said sadly, and he flew away into the dark night.

Psyche threw herself onto the bed and cried until dawn. She waited and waited for him to return. Days stretched into weeks, and weeks into months, but he never came.

When she could bear it no longer, Psyche went to see Venus. "Please help me," she begged.

Venus was still very angry. "You stupid girl," she spat. "How could you think a god would love someone like you? If you want his love back, you must earn it."

"I'll do anything you ask," said Psyche quietly.

Venus took her to a barn. On the floor was a huge pile of corn, rye and barley all mixed together. "Your first task is to separate this grain into three different heaps by the end of the day," she said.

Psyche sat down and began to sort out the grain. After an hour, the pile didn't look any smaller. "It would take me years to finish this," she sobbed.

A few moments later, a line of tiny ants marched across the floor. Psyche watched as one of them picked up a grain, hauled it onto its back and carried it to one of the three tiny heaps. Then, one by one, the other ants did the same.

The little ants scurried to and fro all day. The main pile got smaller and smaller and the little heaps grew and grew, until by evening the grains were all sorted out.

When Venus returned, she wasn't at all pleased. "You haven't finished yet," she said sharply. "Now you must bring me the wool of the golden sheep across the river."

So, the next morning, Psyche hurried down to the river. As she stepped into the water, a reed whispered, "It's too dangerous. The sheep are very vicious. They'll kill you if you try to take their wool."

"What shall I do?" asked Psyche. "I can't go back without it."

"You must wait until noon, when they are resting in the shade," said the reed. "Then you can collect the wool tangled in the bushes by the river."

Psyche did as the reed said and took the wool back to Venus. "You won't find your next task so easy," snapped the goddess. "Take this to the Underworld," she ordered, handing Psyche a box, "and ask Queen Proserpina to send me a little of her beauty."

Poor Psyche didn't even know how to find the Underworld. In despair, she climbed to the top of a tower. Just as she was ready to throw herself off, the tower spoke to her. "There are many dangers ahead," it said, "but if you follow my advice you will be safe."

Psyche listened carefully and then set out on her journey. Bravely, she made her way through the darkest

of caves into the Underworld. When she came to the murky waters of the River Styx, she paid the ferryman Charon, as the tower had said, and they glided across the river in eerie silence.

Charon set Psyche down in front of the palace and her heart almost stopped. Guarding the gates was a huge black dog, with three snarling heads that looked ready to tear her apart.

Psyche tried to keep calm and remember what the tower had said. Quickly, she threw down some bread for the dog and while it was busy eating she slipped inside.

Proserpina welcomed her and laid out a huge banquet, but Psyche didn't touch any of it. The tower had warned her that she would never be able to return if she did. Instead, she sat on the ground and nibbled some dry bread. At the end of the meal, Psyche said shyly, "Do you think you could spare just a little of your beauty to take back to Venus?"

"I don't see why not," said Proserpina and put some in the box. Psyche thanked her and hurried away at once, anxious to spend no more time there than she needed to.

When Psyche emerged from the Underworld and felt the warm glow of the sun, she was filled with relief. She took out the box. The tower had said she mustn't open it. "But what harm can it do?" she thought. "Perhaps a touch of divine beauty would make Cupid love me again." Carefully, Psyche lifted the lid. At once, she slumped to the ground in an everlasting sleep.

When Cupid heard what had happened, he flew to Psyche's side. Gently, he leaned over and blew the sleep out of her eyes. Psyche gazed up at him. "You came back," she whispered.

Cupid kissed her. "I did, and after this I will never leave you again," he said, "but first there's something I need to do. I won't be long."

He flew up to see Jupiter, the most powerful of all the gods. "I want to marry Psyche," he said, "but I can't because she is a mortal."

"Leave it to me," said Jupiter, and he sent for Venus and Psyche. As Psyche knelt before him, he handed her a golden cup – the cup of immortality. "Drink this," he said kindly. Psyche did as she was told and drained every last drop from the cup.

Then Jupiter called Venus to him. "Now they may be married," he said sternly, and, before she could object, he called all the gods and goddesses together for a magnificent wedding feast.

Folk tales
from
around
the
world

The stolen sun

Mokele looked up at the sky. It was dull and dreary again. "Why doesn't the sun ever shine here?" he said to his father.

Chief Wai looked at Mokele sadly. "It did once," he said, "but it was stolen away a long time ago by Chief Mokulaka, who wanted it all for himself."

"Don't be sad, Father," said Mokele. "I'll go and get the sun back for you."

Mokele set to work at once. He cut down a large tree and hollowed it out to make a canoe. While he was busy working, some wasps flew up to him. "Can we come with you?" they buzzed excitedly. "If the chief won't give the sun back, we could sting him."

"Please do," said Mokele, delighted to have some company for his journey.

A little while later, a tortoise crawled up. "Can I come with you?" she grunted. "I'm very good at looking for things. I'll find the sun wherever it's hidden."

"Why not?" said Mokele. "The more the merrier."

A kite heard him and swooped down. "In that case, can I come too?" he said. "I can see better than anyone. I'm sure I could help."

"That would be useful," said Mokele.

Soon, so many animals were crowded into the canoe that there was only just room for Mokele. He climbed in at the back and they set off down the river to find the sun.

For days, they paddled down the river until, at last, they came to the land of Chief Mokulaka. It was just as gloomy there as it was at home.

Mokele climbed out of the canoe and walked straight up to the chief, who was waiting on the riverbank to meet the strangers. "I am the son of Chief Wai," Mokele said politely. "It's always dark in our village and we miss the sun very much. Please may I buy it back from you? We could put it in the sky again and everyone could share it."

Chief Mokulaka frowned. He didn't want to sell the sun, but as he was just about to say so he heard a menacing growl from the canoe. He turned to find a leopard staring at him hungrily. "Very well," he said to Mokele, with a nervous cough, "but I'll need some time to think about a fair price. Why don't you go and rest for a while?"

"All right," said Mokele, and he and the animals climbed out of the canoe and settled down beneath a large tree.

Meanwhile, Chief Mokulaka hurried to see his daughter, Molumba. "This young man has come to take the sun away," he said angrily. "We must kill him. Brew up some poison at once."

He didn't notice a wasp hovering right by them. The wasp heard everything and flew back to warn Mokele about what the chief was planning.

When the chief invited Mokele into Molumba's hut, Mokele pretended he knew nothing about the poison and chatted away with ease.

Molumba liked him so much that secretly she poured the poison away.

While they were all talking, the animals were busy searching for the sun. They looked behind every bush and left no stone unturned, but it was so long since they'd seen it that they could hardly remember what it looked like.

As the tortoise crawled slowly up and down, she saw a golden glow coming from a cave. She went a little closer and felt a delicious warmth spread over her. Closing her eyes, she swayed her head happily. "Surely this must be the sun," she thought.

Gripping the sun tightly, the tortoise began to drag it outside. The keen-eyed kite saw her struggling with it and called the other animals over to help. Suddenly, they heard a shout. They looked up and saw Mokele being chased by Chief Mokulaka and his warriors.

"Leave this to us," buzzed the wasps, and they swarmed over and stung them until they howled with pain and ran away.

In all the chaos, Mokele and the animals hadn't noticed that the sun was no longer lying on the ground. Then a quiet voice said, "Look." Molumba stepped out of the bushes and pointed up at the sky. Mokele and the animals gazed up in awe. The sun was rising, all by itself.

Mokele turned to Molumba. "Our work here is done," he said. "Now we must go home. Will you come with us?"

Molumba nodded shyly. Together, they and the animals hurried back to the canoe and set off up the river.

When they arrived at Mokele's village, everyone was waiting on the riverbank, cheering loudly. They were delighted to have the sun back to light up their lives.

Mokele and Molumba became inseparable. It wasn't long before they were married, and on their wedding day the sun shone the brightest of all.

78

Baba Yaga

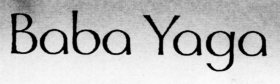

Misha lived with her father and stepmother on the edge of a huge, dark forest. Her stepmother hated her. When Misha's father was there, she pretended to be sweet and kind, but as soon as he left she became cruel and nasty. "Scrub the floors, wretched creature," she would yell, "and don't you *dare* stop until I tell you."

Misha worked from morning until night, cleaning and cooking, washing and ironing. Her stepmother only gave her scraps of dry bread and cheese to eat, and Misha grew thin and pale. But, she was too scared of her stepmother to tell her father what was happening.

One morning, the stepmother shouted to Misha, "I want to do some sewing, but I haven't any needles. You must go to my sister who lives in the forest, and ask her to lend me some. Go at once, you lazy girl."

Misha was very scared. Her stepmother's sister was even more horrible than she was. She was a hideous witch called Baba Yaga, with a long pointy nose and extraordinary iron teeth.

"I'll go," said Misha meekly, but first she hurried to her real aunt's house to ask for her advice. Her aunt listened carefully and when Misha had finished she nodded wisely. Then she bustled around gathering things

from her cupboards. "You'll need these," she said matter of factly. "Feed the cat and the dog, tie the ribbon to the birch tree and don't forget to oil the hinges of the gate."

"Thank you," said Misha. She tied the things up in her handkerchief and set off for Baba Yaga's house.

As she walked through the forest, Misha glanced nervously around her. "There might be wolves and bears here," she thought fearfully.

Misha walked faster and faster, until she was almost running. At last, she reached Baba Yaga's house. It was the strangest house she had ever seen. It had legs like a chicken's and was surrounded by a fence made of bones and skulls. Misha took a deep breath and pushed open the gate. It creaked loudly.

At that moment, she heard a noise behind her. She turned and saw Baba Yaga hurtling through the trees in a huge mortar, steering it with a pestle. She was going so fast that she almost crashed right into Misha. "What do you want?" she screeched.

Misha was trembling with fright, but she tried to keep her voice steady. "Your sister sent me to borrow some needles," she managed to say.

"Did she? Did she indeed?" said Baba Yaga thoughtfully. "Well, you'd better come inside." She muttered something that Misha couldn't hear. The house stood up on its chicken legs and spun around to face them. Then it crashed to the ground and the door flew open.

Misha's heart pounded, but it was too late to turn back, so she followed Baba Yaga inside. "I'll give you the needles after supper," said Baba Yaga. Her iron teeth glinted as she grinned greedily at Misha. "But first I'm going to have a bath. You can do some weaving while you're waiting." With that, she marched into the bathhouse and slammed the door behind her.

Misha stepped back and almost tripped over Baba Yaga's cat. It snarled and spat at her. "Poor thing," said Misha gently. "You look half-starved." She opened her handkerchief and gave it a piece of cheese. The cat ate it up at once.

Misha smiled. "You were hungry," she said. The cat purred softly as Misha stroked its back. Then it sat up and stared at her intently. "Misha, you must go now or you'll never escape. Baba Yaga will eat you for supper," it meowed. "I'll do the weaving, so Baba Yaga will hear the loom clacking away and think you're working it. Take this towel and this comb. When Baba Yaga comes after you, throw down the towel first and then the comb. Now go, quickly."

"Thank you, thank you," whispered Misha, and she grabbed the needles for her stepmother and hurried to the door. As she opened it, a thin dog ran at her, growling fiercely. "You look hungry too," said Misha. Quickly, she untied her handkerchief, and gave the dog a bone. She watched as it gnawed at the bone eagerly. When the dog had finished, it gave her a grateful look and let her pass.

As Misha ran down the steps, the branches of a birch tree snatched at her clothes, as if trying to stop her from escaping. She fumbled in her handkerchief and brought out a yellow ribbon. Carefully, she tied it around the branch in a neat bow and the branch sprang out of her way.

Misha raced down the path and was just about to fling open the gate when she remembered what her aunt had said. She opened her handkerchief, took out the oil and squeezed a few drops onto the gate's hinges. It opened without so much as a squeak. The way was clear. Misha raced through the forest as fast as her legs would carry her.

In the strange little house, Baba Yaga shouted from the bathtub, "Are you weaving, my dear?"

The cat worked the loom, clackety-clack, clackety-clack. "Yes, Baba Yaga," she meowed, trying to sound like Misha.

Baba Yaga raised an eyebrow suspiciously. Something wasn't right. She rushed out of the bathhouse and, when she saw the cat sitting at the loom, she let out a shriek. "Traitor! Why did you let that girl escape?" she wailed.

The cat stared at Baba Yaga. "I've worked for you for years and years, but you were never as kind to me as Misha was." Baba Yaga tried to kick the cat, but it jumped out of the window, and disappeared into the forest.

Baba Yaga ran to the door and flung it open. When she saw the dog, she shrieked, "What about you? Why didn't you bark to warn me she was getting away?"

The dog looked at her. "I've worked for you for years and years, but you never gave me anything. Misha was kind to me and gave me a bone with meat on it."

"You never gave me anything either," added the birch tree. "Misha gave me a lovely yellow ribbon."

"And she oiled my hinges," piped up the gate.

"Bah! I don't need you. I'll get her myself. She won't escape from me," screamed Baba Yaga. Gnashing her iron teeth with rage, she climbed into her mortar and crashed through the forest after Misha.

Misha ran as fast as she could, but soon she heard Baba Yaga chasing after her. When the witch had almost caught up, Misha stopped and threw down the towel the cat had given her. At once, a great, wide river appeared between them. The mortar was too heavy to fly so far. Baba Yaga leaped out and jumped up and down, waving her fists in frustration. "You won't get away that easily," she shouted after Misha.

While Misha ran on through the forest, Baba Yaga went back to her house and drove her herd of cows down to the river.

The thirsty cows drank up all the water, and soon Baba Yaga was able to bump over the dry riverbed in her mortar.

When Misha heard the mortar chasing after her again, she threw down the comb. At once, a thorn forest sprang up. Baba Yaga jumped out of her mortar, and tried to chew the trees down with her iron teeth. But they weren't strong enough. The forest was so thick and tangled that nothing could get through it.

"AAAAAAAAAARGH!" screamed Baba Yaga. She knew that she was defeated. Misha had escaped.

Misha ran and ran until she could run no more. Wearily, she stumbled on. Then, at last, she saw her father's house between the trees. As she got closer, she saw to her delight that her father was standing outside waiting for her.

She ran into his arms. "Misha, Misha, where have you been?" he cried, hugging her. "I was so worried about you."

Through her tears, Misha told him about her stepmother and Baba Yaga, and everything that had happened.

Her father was horrified. "I had no idea what a horrible woman your stepmother was," he said. "But there's no need to worry any more. I'll see she gets what she deserves."

The stepmother saw all of this through the window and decided it was time to go. Very quietly, she crept out through the back door.

From that day on, Misha lived very happily with her father in their house at the edge of the forest. Baba Yaga never came near them and Misha's wicked stepmother was never seen again.

Sister Lace

In a tiny village in the mountains, there lived a beautiful girl known as Sister Lace. Of course, that wasn't her real name, but everyone called her Sister Lace because of the exquisite lace that she wove. She was so skilled that people would come from miles around just to watch her.

Her fingers danced to and fro like butterflies in a summer breeze. She embroidered flowers so lifelike you could almost smell their scent, animals so convincing they looked ready to leap out at you and birds so intricate they nearly sang aloud. Even delicate spiders' webs sparkling in the morning dew looked clumsy beside her work. She wove pretty collars and cuffs, elaborate tablecloths and bedspreads, elegant shawls and veils — anything that anyone asked her to make.

Eventually, word of Sister Lace's talent reached the emperor, who called for his general. "Why haven't I heard of this girl before?" he demanded. "Bring her here at once."

So the general took three soldiers and set off that very day to search for Sister Lace. They rode through the kingdom and over the mountains until they reached her village. "Where is this girl who makes beautiful lace?" asked the general.

The villagers couldn't imagine what the emperor's soldiers might want with Sister Lace, but they showed them where they could find her.

Sister Lace was sitting on the porch when the general and his soldiers marched over. "Can I help you?" she said, surprised to have such important visitors.

"You must come with us now," barked the general. "The emperor wants to see you."

Sister Lace shook her head. "This is my home," she said quietly, "and I do not want to see the emperor."

"What?" spluttered the general. "How dare you disobey the emperor. Men, seize her!" he ordered.

The soldiers didn't move. He turned to find them standing in a row and staring, utterly captivated by the movement of Sister Lace's nimble fingers. "Wake up!" he snapped.

The soldiers blinked and looked around in confusion. "I said seize her!" yelled the general.

This time, the soldiers did as they were told, and carried Sister Lace away to the court of the emperor. "Welcome," said the emperor, as they brought her before him. "I hope you like your new home."

"This is not my home," she said defiantly.

"Don't worry. You'll soon get used to it," he said.

Sister Lace bowed her head as if to kiss his hand, but instead she bared her teeth and sank them into it as hard as she could.

"Yooooooooow!" shrieked the emperor, snatching his hand away. His face flushed red with pain and rage. "Take her away and lock her up," he commanded.

The next morning, Sister Lace was brought before the emperor again. "You must stop this silliness," he said firmly. "I've decided to forgive you and make you my wife."

"I'd rather die than marry you," gasped Sister Lace in absolute horror.

"I'm sure that can be arranged," piped up one of his advisors. "You should have her executed for such impudence," he said to the emperor.

"Fool!" yelled the emperor. "After all the trouble I've had to bring her here, is this the advice you give me? It's you who should be executed. Get out of here. Now, has anyone got any better ideas?"

Another advisor crept forward nervously and whispered in the emperor's ear. The emperor nodded in approval and turned to Sister Lace. "I've heard all about the amazing lace you weave," he said. "If you can make me a live rooster out of lace, I'll let you go home. If not, you must stay here with me. You've got seven days."

In her dark prison cell, Sister Lace wept the night away, but when morning came she dried her tears and set to work. Day and night, night and day she worked, not sleeping a wink. She worked so fast that her fingers bled.

By the time the sun's rays streamed through the bars of the window on the seventh morning, Sister Lace had made a beautiful lace rooster. As she picked it up, her fingers smeared the rooster's comb with blood. It wasn't alive, but it looked just like a real rooster.

Sister Lace hung her head sadly. A large tear rolled down her cheek and splashed into the rooster's mouth. To her complete surprise, the bird sprang to life and crowed to welcome the morning.

Suddenly, the cell door flew open and in burst the emperor. When he saw the rooster strutting up and down, he stopped in his tracks. He stared at Sister Lace in amazement. Then a suspicious look crept across his face. "You've cheated!" he exclaimed. "That's not made of lace at all. It's just one of the palace roosters. You'll have to do better than that. I'll give you seven more days. This time, you must make me a partridge. If you can do that, I will allow you to go home."

When the rooster heard the emperor's words, it was so disgusted that it flew at him and scratched his head with its claws. "Poor, poor Sister Lace," it said. "How I hate the emperor." With that, it flapped past the emperor and out of the open door.

The emperor stormed away in a fury, dabbing his bleeding head with his handkerchief.

Sister Lace's eyes filled with tears. It seemed hopeless, but she bowed her head and set to work once more. Day and night, her fingers threaded and twisted, looped and spun. No matter how tired she became, she kept on going, desperately hoping to please the emperor so she could escape.

At last, just as the seventh morning began to dawn, Sister Lace laid down the lace partridge. She stroked the bird softly with her bleeding fingers, leaving a smear of blood on its breast and a pattern of red speckles on its feathers. "Poor little thing," she said gently. "Do you hate this prison too?" As she spoke, a tear trickled from the corner of her eye and splashed into the partridge's mouth. Instantly, the partridge fluttered its wings and began to fly around the room.

At that moment, the emperor arrived. "What's this?" he blustered when he saw the partridge. "That's not what I asked for. I wanted…errr…a dragon. I'll give you one more chance," he said, "but if you can't make me a dragon within seven days you must stay here forever."

On hearing these words, the partridge flew at the emperor and scratched his neck. "Poor, poor Sister Lace," it said. "How I hate the emperor." And, with that, it flew over the emperor's head and out through the door.

With his pride wounded as much as his head and neck, the emperor stomped out of the cell.

91

Sister Lace was exhausted by now, but you would never have guessed. She worked harder than ever, hoping with all her heart that this time the emperor would allow her to go free.

By the time dawn had turned the sky rosy-pink on the seventh morning, Sister Lace had made a small but exquisitely formed lace dragon. She looked at it and sighed. Blood from her sore fingers had soaked into the lace, turning it fiery red. "It's no use, my little dragon," wept Sister Lace. "The emperor will only go back on his word again. I don't think he'll ever let me go home."

As her tears fell into the dragon's mouth, it gave a little wriggle and burst into life. At that very second, the emperor arrived. When he saw the dragon, he stepped back in alarm, even though it was so small. "That's not a dragon!" he exclaimed. "It's...errr...a snake."

The little red dragon swelled with indignation. It grew and grew until it was bigger than a tiger and then, opening its mouth wide, it shot forth a ball of flames.

Soon, the entire palace was ablaze. The emperor and his advisors ran for their lives, leaving Sister Lace alone with the dragon. "Poor, poor Sister Lace," it said. "Let's get out of here." She climbed onto its back and the dragon swooped out through the prison door and up into the sky. In no time at all, the flaming palace was far behind them. Sister Lace was on her way home.

The musicians of Bremen

For many years, the donkey had worked hard for his master, but now he was old and tired. "I'm no longer needed here," he thought sadly. So, early one morning, he set off down the road to Bremen, to become a musician in the town band.

After a little way, the donkey saw an old hunting dog lying by the side of the road. As he passed, it gave a heavy sigh. The donkey stopped. "What's the matter, my friend?" he said.

"I'm too old to hunt any more, so my master beats me," said the dog. "I've run away from him, but now I'm starving."

"I'm going to Bremen to play in the town band," said the donkey. "Why don't you come with me? I'll play the trombone and you can bang on the drum."

The dog thought for a moment. "You know, I think I will," he said, and together they trotted away down the road to Bremen.

A little further on, they came across a cat that looked very miserable indeed.

"Why such a long face?" asked the donkey.

"I'm too old to catch mice," mewed the cat. "My mistress threatened to drown me because I'm no use, so I ran away, and now I don't know what to do."

"We're going to Bremen to play in the town band," said the donkey. "Why don't you come with us? I'm going to play the trombone, the dog's going to bang on the drum and you could play the fiddle."

"I think I will," said the cat, so together the donkey, the dog and the cat trotted away down the road to Bremen. As they passed by a farmyard, a loud "COCK-A-DOODLE-DOO" almost made them jump out of their skin. They looked up and saw a rooster standing on a wall.

"What's all that noise about?" said the donkey. "You frightened us half to death."

"I'm crowing while I still can," replied the rooster mournfully. "Tomorrow, there are important guests arriving, and my mistress has told the cook to make me into soup for their dinner."

"We're going to Bremen to play in the town band," said the donkey. "You have a fine loud voice. Why don't you come with us, and we can all make music?"

"Well, it certainly beats being made into soup," said the rooster, so together the donkey, the dog, the cat and the rooster trotted away down the road to Bremen.

It was a long way to Bremen, and the four friends still hadn't reached the town when it began to grow dark. They kept on going for a while, but then they came to a big forest. "It's no good. We'll have to stay here for the night," said the donkey, and he lay down under a tree. The dog stretched out beside him on a pile of dry leaves.

"I'll sleep up here," purred the cat, and she climbed the tree and curled up on a branch.

"I think I'll join you," said the rooster, and he flew up to the top of the tree.

The rooster was just closing
his eyes when he saw a faint glimmer of light through
the trees. "I think I can see a house," he said excitedly.

The cat blinked at him with her big, green eyes. "Well,
what are we waiting for?" she mewed. "It's got to be more
comfortable than here. Let's go."

The dog jumped up and shook off the leaves. "Great idea,"
he panted eagerly. "I could do with a good dinner."

The donkey, the dog, the cat and the rooster hurried
through the forest in the direction of the light. Soon, they
came to a small cottage. It was a welcome sight to the four
tired, hungry animals.

The donkey was the tallest, so he went up to the window
and peered inside. "What can you see?" growled the dog softly.

"It's a robber's den," whispered the donkey. "There's a big
pile of gold in the corner and there are four men sitting at
a table piled high with delicious-looking food."

The dog licked his lips hungrily. "Mmmm. That would suit
us very well indeed, but what are we going to do about the
robbers?" he asked.

"We'll have to think of a plan," said the donkey. "Has anybody got any ideas?"

The four friends put their heads together and whispered to one another. At last, the donkey straightened up. "That's a very good plan," he said. "Now, you all know what to do. Don't make a sound until I give the signal."

Very quietly, the donkey reared up on his hind legs. Then the dog jumped up on the donkey's back, the cat climbed onto the dog's back and the rooster flew up and perched on top of the cat. "Are you ready?" whispered the donkey.

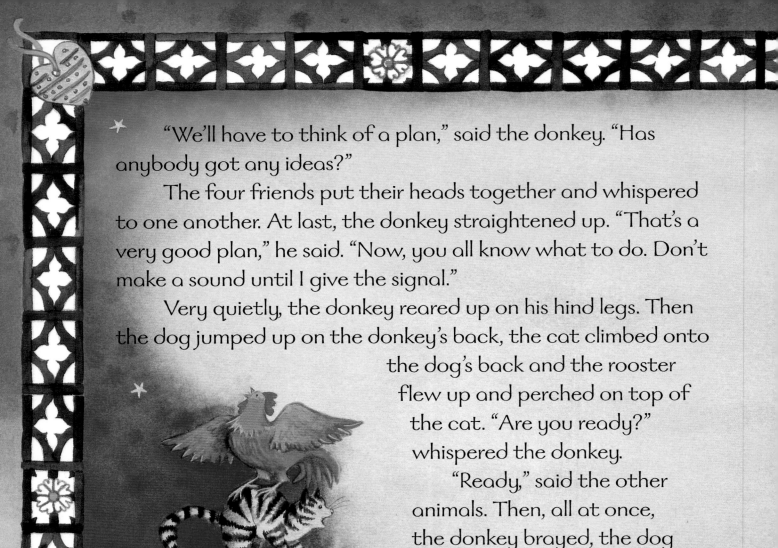

"Ready," said the other animals. Then, all at once, the donkey brayed, the dog barked, the cat meowed and the rooster crowed as loudly as they possibly could.

In the cottage, the robbers shot out of their chairs, terrified by the deafening noise. "Let's get out of here," cried one, and they rushed out of the door, pushing and shoving each other to get out first.

The four animals chuckled to themselves as the robbers fled into the forest. When they were sure they had gone, the animals trotted into the cottage and ate all that was left on the table. Then, tired out, they turned out the light and settled down to sleep. The donkey lay down on some straw in the yard, the dog stretched out behind the door, the cat curled up in front of the hearth, and the rooster perched on a beam. Within a few minutes, they were all fast asleep.

Out in the forest, the robbers saw the light go out. Everything was still and quiet. "We shouldn't have been so scared," said the leader. "Go back and find out what's happening," he ordered one of the men.

The robber crept through the trees to the cottage. When he reached the door, he stopped and listened. He couldn't hear anything, so he pushed it open and tiptoed inside. In the darkness, he saw the cat's eyes glowing and thought they were hot coals from the fire. As he bent down to blow them into a flame, the cat spat at him and scratched his face with her claws.

The robber jumped up, terrified. He fumbled for the door and tripped over the dog, who bit his leg. As he fled into the yard, he ran into the donkey, who gave him a good, hard kick. Of course, all of this noise disturbed the rooster, who woke up with a start and cried out "cock-a-doodle-doo".

The man ran back to the other robbers. "There's a horrible witch in the cottage," he gasped. "She spat at me and scratched my face with her long nails. Then one of her servants stabbed me with a knife and another hit me with a club. When I ran out of the cottage, I heard one of them shout, 'Crook, what do you do?'"

The other robbers stared at him, wide-eyed with fear. They didn't dare go back to the cottage, even in daylight. In fact they never, ever went back there again.

The donkey, the dog, the cat and the rooster never did join the town band in Bremen. Instead, they stayed happily in the cottage and, for all anyone knows, the four friends may be living there still.

Brave Hendrick

As Hendrick was hurrying home from school one afternoon, he decided to take a short cut. He ran along the top of one of the great dykes that protected Holland's low-lying farmland from the sea. Hendrick loved the peaceful sound of the waves lapping against the dykes. It made him feel safe.

But tonight he heard an unfamiliar sound too – the gentle trickle of water. He stopped and listened for a moment. "That doesn't sound right," thought Hendrick. "I'd better have a look."

He scrambled down the dyke and ran along it until he found where the noise was coming from. There was a small hole in the dyke and water was spurting through it.

Now, this might not seem very important to you, but Hendrick knew how serious a leak in a dyke could be. His grandfather had helped to build the dykes and his father still worked on them, mending any holes or cracks. "We must watch the dykes," his father had often told him. "If the sea broke through, it would drown all the animals, flood our houses and ruin our farms."

Even a tiny hole like this could spell disaster. Soon, the tide would come in and the force of the waves would make the hole bigger and bigger until the waves crashed right through. He looked around for someone to tell, but there was no one in sight. "Help!" he shouted, as loudly as he could.

There was no answer. Hendrick stared at the hole, wondering what to do. "If I run home and tell my father, it might be too late by the time he gets here," he said to himself. "I must do something now. But what?"

He rummaged in his pockets for a handkerchief or something to stuff into the hole, but his pockets were empty. Suddenly, Hendrick looked at his hands. "Perfect!" he thought, and he pushed his finger into the hole. Instantly, the water stopped trickling through. He had fixed the leak, for the moment at least. Hendrick was filled with relief. Leaning against the dyke, he shouted again. "Help! Help!"

Nobody came. Hendrick kept on shouting until he was hoarse, but the only answer was the sound of the waves crashing against the dyke. The nearest houses were much too far away for anyone to hear. He was all alone.

As the wind howled around him, he shivered. The water was freezing cold too and he could no longer feel his finger. "It must be blue by now," he thought miserably.

It was growing dark and Hendrick began to feel scared. He didn't know how long he had been crouching there, but it felt like an eternity. He could hear the sea thundering against the dyke, trying to get through. "Please help me," he cried, but he knew it was no use.

Hendrick's mind began to wander. He thought of his warm,

snug house, and his mother getting his supper ready. A tear trickled down his cold face. He rubbed it away roughly with his spare hand. "I'm not giving up," he said aloud.

Shivering with cold, Hendrick wrapped his coat tighter around him. "Mother and Father must have missed me by now," he told himself. "They're bound to come looking for me soon." But then he began to panic. "How will they find me? I don't usually come this way. They won't even know where to look."

It grew darker and darker and still no one came. Hours passed, but they seemed like weeks to poor Hendrick. His whole body grew numb with cold, and he wasn't sure he could move any more. "Whatever happens, I must keep the water out," he whispered firmly to himself.

Then, at last, Hendrick saw a light moving in the distance. "Over here," he called, but as soon as the words were out of his mouth they were snatched away by the wind.

As the light carried on past him, Hendrick's heart sank. "Oh help! Please help me," he called in desperation. His voice was so faint it was almost impossible to hear it, but miraculously the light stopped and it began to bob along the dyke. "Who's there?" came a voice a few moments later.

"It's me, Hendrick," was the faint reply.

A man's kindly face peered over the edge of the dyke, lit up by the yellow glow from the lantern. He was shocked to see Hendrick crouching there. "What's a little lad like you doing out here on a night like this?" he said.

"I'm plugging the dyke to keep out the water," said the exhausted Hendrick.

"Are you now?" said the man, climbing down to have a look. Hendrick showed him the hole and told him all about the trickle of water.

"You did well to hold it back for so long," said the man. "I dread to think what would have happened if you hadn't found it. Hold on just a little longer and I'll get help."

At that moment, they heard voices calling. They looked up and saw the lights of lots more lanterns bobbing busily along the dyke, like curious fireflies.

Hendrick recognized one of the voices. "That's my father," he said weakly, and he was right. Hendrick's father and uncle, and many men from the village were all out searching for him.

"Over here!" shouted the man, and he climbed up on the dyke and waved to them. Hendrick's father saw him and hurried over. "Quick, your lad's down here," said the man, and told him what had happened.

Hendrick's father rushed down and wrapped his coat around the shivering boy. "I had to keep the water out," said Hendrick, his finger still in the hole.

"You're a very brave boy, and I'm proud of you," said his father. "You did just the right thing. Without you, the whole village could have been lost."

"That's right," said Hendrick's uncle, climbing down to join them. "Now, don't you worry about the dyke. We'll soon have it fixed and it will be as good as new, thanks to you."

Hendrick's father eased his son's icy finger out of the hole. Then he lifted him up in his strong arms and carried him home.

As Hendrick snuggled down in bed, he felt a warm glow of pride. The village was safe again.

Puss in boots

Once there was an old miller who had three sons. When he died, the miller left his mill to the eldest son, his donkey to the second son, and to the youngest son, he left his cat.

The two eldest sons were pleased with what their father had left to them. Together, they could earn a good living with the mill and the donkey. But the youngest son was not so happy. "It's all right for them," he grumbled, "but all I have is a useless cat. I'll starve to death."

"Master," purred the cat, "I'm not useless. Just give me a sack and a pair of boots, and you'll soon see how useful I can be."

The young man stared at the cat in astonishment. He had only ever seen the cat chasing mice and now here it was talking to him. "Well, I never," he said. "Whoever heard of a talking cat?" He couldn't imagine how the cat could be useful to him, but he decided to do as it asked, and went to the village to find a sack and have a pair of boots made. "I must be crazy wasting the only money I have on these," he thought.

When he returned, the cat put on the boots and stood upright. "Leave everything to me, master," it said, and marched away with the sack over its shoulder.

The cat found a grassy hill full of rabbit burrows. It filled the sack with fresh, juicy leaves and left it open on the ground. Then it hid behind a bush and waited.

Soon, a curious rabbit peered out of a hole and sniffed the air. It bounded eagerly over to the sack and hopped inside to munch on the leaves. Immediately, the cat leaped out and grabbed the sack with the rabbit inside. Then, slinging the sack over its shoulder, it set off for the king's palace.

When the cat came before the king, it bowed down low and said, "Your Majesty, I bring you a gift from my master, the Marquis de Carabas."

"How remarkable," thought the king. He had seen many weird and wonderful things on his travels, but never a talking cat. "It's really very kind of your master. Please thank him for his gift," he said, and sent the rabbit to the kitchens to be cooked for his dinner.

The next day, the cat presented the king with a pair of partridges. The king beamed with pleasure. "How generous of your master to think of me again," he said.

Every day, the cat took something that it had caught to the king. One day it was a pheasant, another day it was huge fish, and another day it was an entire wild boar. Each time, the cat bowed down low and said, "A gift from the Marquis de Carabas, Your Majesty."

The king was delighted with his gifts and each time he asked the cat to thank its master.

Now, the king had an exceptionally beautiful daughter and the cat had a clever plan. One morning, when it knew that the king was out in his carriage with the princess, the cat ran to get the miller's son. "Quick, come with me," it said.

"Why? Where are we going?" said the miller's son.

"Never mind that," said the cat. "Just do as I tell you." It led him to a lake near a road. "Take off your clothes and jump into the water," it ordered. "When you hear a carriage coming, you must shout and splash and pretend you can't swim. Leave the rest to me."

The miller's son thought the cat had lost its mind, but it spoke with such authority that he did as he was told.

A little while later the king's carriage came rumbling along the road. The cat ran up to it, crying, "Help! My master, the Marquis de Carabas, is drowning."

"Why, it's the cat that brings me all the gifts," said the king. "We must help its master." The carriage jerked to a halt, and the king ordered his servants to rescue the man in the water.

It wasn't long before the miller's son was safely on the bank, wrapped in a cloak. "Your Majesty," said the cat, "this is rather embarrassing. The Marquis de Carabas's clothes have been stolen. He has nothing to wear!"

The king immediately sent his servants to the palace to fetch some clothes. They brought back a splendid suit, cloak, hat and shoes. When the miller's son put them on, he looked most handsome. He bowed to the princess, and she smiled and blushed. "You must ride in my carriage," said the king to the miller's son. "We'll take you home."

Meanwhile, the cat ran on ahead. It came to a field where people were hard at work harvesting. "The king is coming this way," the cat said to them. "When he asks who owns this land, say it belongs to the Marquis de Carabas, or I'll turn you into mincemeat."

Sure enough, as the king passed by, he called out to the harvesters, "Who owns this land?"

"The Marquis de Carabas," they replied, just as the cat had ordered. The king was most impressed and smiled at the miller's son, who tried not to look astonished at his new wealth.

Once more, the cat ran on ahead. It came to a magnificent castle, which was home to a huge ogre. The cat wasn't at all afraid. It marched up to it and strode inside.

The ogre peered at the cat suspiciously. "What do you want?" he growled, not used to having visitors.

"I'm here to pay my respects," purred the cat politely. "I have heard that you can turn yourself into any animal you like, even a lion. I couldn't quite believe it, so I came to see it with my own eyes."

At once, the ogre turned into a huge lion, with a great, shaggy mane. It opened its mouth and gave a deafening roar, revealing a set of enormous, razor-sharp teeth.

This was too much even for the bold little cat. It shot up to the top of the curtains, where it stayed, shivering with fright, until the lion stopped roaring and turned back into an ogre.

"Now do you believe it?" said the ogre, beaming proudly.

"I certainly do," said the cat. "It's really very clever of you. I suppose, as you're so large already, it can't be difficult to turn yourself into a great big lion. But I bet you can't make yourself into something really small, such as a mouse. Surely that would be impossible."

"Of course I can," said the ogre indignantly. "Nothing is impossible for me." A moment later, the huge ogre had shrunk to a tiny mouse. "See?" it squeaked, as it scampered around on the floor.

"Oh yes," said the cat, with a menacing glint in its eye. "I see all right." Then, as quick as a flash, it pounced on the mouse and ate it up.

The cat was just licking its lips as the king's carriage drew up. It hurried outside to meet them. "Welcome to the castle of the Marquis de Carabas," it said with a bow.

The miller's son stepped out of the carriage and gazed up at the castle in awe. The cat nudged him. "Remember, you're supposed to be the Marquis de Carabas," it hissed. "Try to behave like him."

"What? Oh, yes, of course," said the miller's son, and he turned to help the princess down from the carriage. Her pretty eyes sparkled like stardust, and his heart leaped as she took his hand. "The princess would be a lovely wife for me," he thought dreamily.

The king stepped down from the carriage too and he nodded in satisfaction when he saw the castle and the land and farms all around it.

"Do come inside," said the cat with a bow. "Lunch is served." It led them through the castle gates and into a grand hall. Stretched out before them on long tables was a wonderful feast that the ogre had prepared for himself.

"The Marquis de Carabas must be very rich," thought the king. "He would make an excellent husband for my daughter."

And since everyone was in perfect agreement about what a wonderful couple they would make, the Marquis de Carabas and the princess were soon married. They lived very happily together in the castle, and the cat lived with them, having shown beyond doubt just how useful it could be. And it never again had to chase a mouse, unless, of course, it couldn't think of anything better to do!

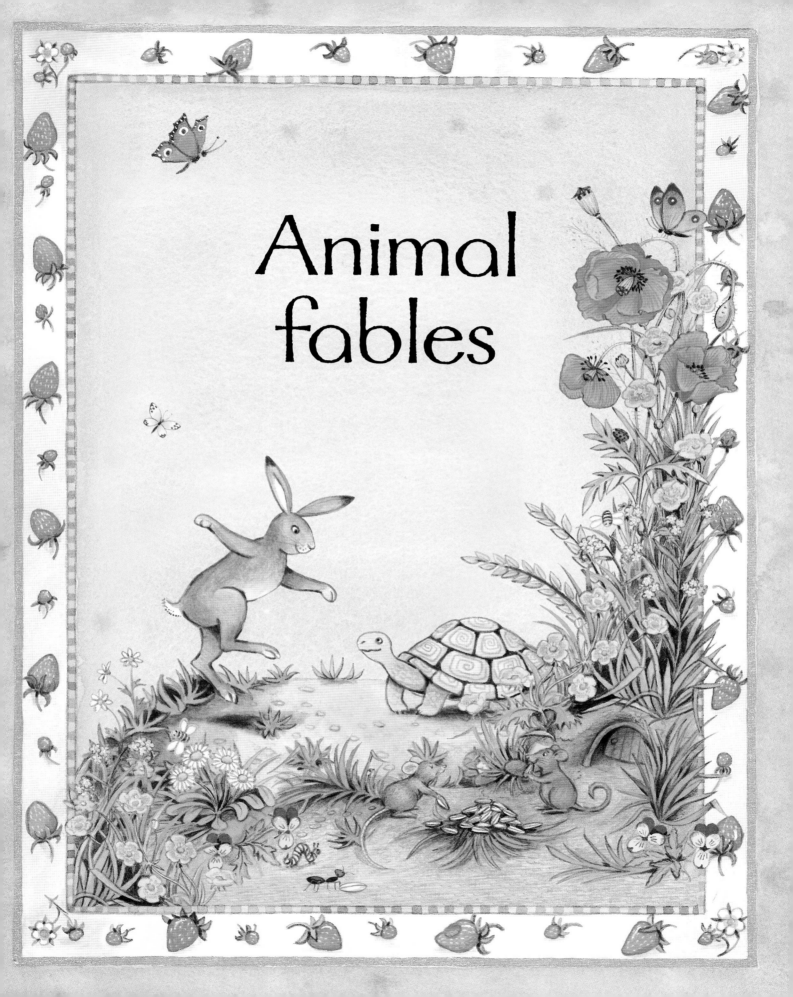

Animal
fables

The stork who outfoxed a fox

In the woods by the lake, there lived a sly fox. He was well known for playing practical jokes, and he was rather proud of his reputation too. But because the animals in the woods knew the fox so well, none of them fell for his tricks any more. Whenever he invited them for dinner or told them anything unusual, the animals would just laugh and say to one other, "Pay no attention. He's just trying to fool us."

One afternoon, the fox saw a stork land by the edge of the lake. "We have a newcomer," he remarked to some squirrels who were scurrying around in the branches overhead. "I think I'll go and welcome her to the area."

"Don't think you can trick a stork," warned the squirrels. "Storks are very clever birds. They wouldn't fall for your tricks."

"Oh, don't you think so?" said the fox. "Well, just watch this." He sauntered out of the trees and strolled up to the stork.

"Good afternoon to you," he said politely.

"Good afternoon," replied the stork, peering down her long beak at the fox.

"I haven't seen you before," said the fox casually. "Are you new around here?"

"Yes," replied the stork. "In fact, I've flown a very long way. I'm just stopping here for a few days' rest."

"Oh really?" said the fox. "Well, allow me to be the first to welcome you." He cocked his head to one side and gave a wide, crafty smile. "In these woods," he continued, "we usually share our food with newcomers. Could I invite you to dinner?"

The stork looked delighted. "Thank you," she said. "That's very kind."

"I'll just go and get some food ready then," said the fox. "Why don't you come over in about an hour?"

"Very well," nodded the stork.

"You'll find my door beneath the big oak tree," said the fox, and he trotted off into the woods.

When the stork arrived for dinner, the fox was very polite. "Welcome," he said, and brought out a big, shallow dish of steaming vegetable soup. The stork's stomach rumbled hungrily.

"It's our custom to eat from the same dish," said the fox as he set it down on the table. "Is that all right with you?"

"Of course," said the stork.

"Splendid," replied the fox. "Do help yourself."

The stork dipped her beak into the soup to try some. But, because the dish was so shallow and her beak was so long, she could only scoop up the tiniest drop.

The fox, meanwhile, settled down opposite her, and began to lap up the soup with his tongue. The stork watched forlornly as he lapped and lapped.

"Mmmm. It is delicious," murmured the fox, "even if I do say so myself." He glanced at the stork out of the corner of his eye. "Aren't you hungry?" he smirked, and kept on lapping.

The stork tried to eat some more soup. She dipped the tip of her beak in again, but she couldn't scoop any up. Then she tried putting her whole beak in sideways, but it didn't fit. The more soup the fox lapped up, the lower the level dropped and the more difficult it became for the stork to eat. She watched miserably as the fox licked the dish clean.

When the fox had finished the last little drop, he sat back and patted his full belly. He looked at the stork's long face and grinned. "Did you enjoy your dinner?" he asked.

The stork took one look at the fox's smug expression and realized that she'd been tricked. But she pretended not to have noticed. "It was lovely," she said graciously. "Thank you so much."

"The pleasure was all mine," said the fox, trying desperately to keep a straight face.

Later on that night, as the stork waded around in the lake trying to catch some fish to fill her empty belly, she racked her brains for a way to pay the fox back. When, at last, she caught a glistening fish in her long, thin beak, she suddenly had an idea.

In the morning, she went to see the fox. "I'd like to invite you for lunch to repay your kindness," she said.

"Really?" said the fox, looking surprised.

"Yes," said the stork. "Come to the lake at one o'clock. I'll have everything ready."

As she stalked off into the woods, a burst of giggles came from a branch overhead. "Watch out," called a squirrel. "That bird is going to get you back."

The fox shook his head. "No chance of that," he said. "You can't outfox a fox!"

That afternoon, the fox arrived at the lake, ready for his lunch. "Let's use your custom of eating our soup from the same dish," said the stork, and she brought out a tall jar with a long, thin neck. "Do start," she urged the fox. "Don't be shy."

The fox looked at the jar uncertainly. He stood up on his hind legs and rested his paws on the rim. A delicious smell wafted up from the soup and made his mouth water. He stretched his neck and just managed to dip the very tip of his tongue into the soup.

The stork leaned over and slipped her long, thin beak down into the jar. "Delicious," she said, swallowing a large beakful of soup, "even if I do say so myself." She smiled at the fox, who was staring forlornly at the neck of the jar. "Not hungry?" asked the stork innocently.

The fox tried again to dip his tongue into the soup, but he couldn't reach at all now that the stork had eaten some. He licked a couple of drops that had spilled over the side, but that only made him even hungrier. He watched unhappily as the stork finished off every last drop.

Gales of laughter came from a nearby tree. "Serves you right!" scolded the squirrels, who had been watching with glee. "That stork's gone and beaten you at your own game!"

The dancing camel

It was midsummer's eve, and animals from all around the world were making their way to the top of a big, green hill for the midsummer party. Everyone was going – from the tiniest beetle to the most enormous elephant, the scaliest lizard to the furriest bear. The air hummed with excitement as they crawled, trotted, hopped and scurried up the hill.

   "Let the party begin," roared the lion as the last few animals arrived at the top. The band struck up a tune at once. The kangaroo drummed on the ground with her feet, the elephant blew his trumpet, the goose honked, the cricket played his fiddle and the squirrel tooted away on a little wooden pipe.

120

Everyone chattered away cheerfully, catching up on each other's news. Everyone, that is, apart from the camel. The camel was a grumpy old soul. He grumbled away to whoever would listen. "This had better be a good party," he said. "I've come a very long way."

"You're not the only one," said the penguin. "Cheer up, camel. It'll be great — it always is."

The party got off to a wonderful start with all the usual games. The crocodile and the alligator played snap while the others had a game of leapfrog. After pin the tail on the donkey and piggy in the middle, all the animals joined in for hide-and-seek. The chameleon won, of course, as she did every year.

After the games, it was the tradition for each of the animals to entertain the others. This year was more fun than ever before. The dolphin put on a stunning water display, a pair of eagles performed a death-defying airshow and the orangutan did some spectacular acrobatics in the treetops.

Even the grumpy camel joined in, with a little persuasion from the mother kangaroo. He gave all the baby animals rides around the hill on his humps and told thrilling tales of his desert adventures. "Only once a year," he snorted. "Once a year only." But his eyes twinkled with amusement beneath his frown.

The funniest performance by far was the monkey's dance. The band struck up a lively tune and all the animals gathered around to watch. The monkey swung through the treetops in time to the beat, jitterbugged with a family of bats, danced cheek to cheek with a laughing baboon and then tangoed across the grass with a pretty lady skunk.

The audience was utterly captivated. They clapped in time to the music and giggled and gasped at the monkey's daring dance moves.

For his grand finale, the monkey sprang high into the air, turned a triple somersault, and landed gracefully on the tip of the elephant's trunk.

All the animals cheered, clapped and hollered for more. Apart from one. "Harrumph!" snorted the camel. "I don't know why you're all clapping so hard. Anyone can dance like that."

"Don't be such an old grumpy humps," chided the mother kangaroo. "The monkey was doing what he's good at, and we should all cheer him for it. You should be happy doing what you're good at, rather than envying him. Camels can't dance."

"Of course they can," grunted the camel.

"Oh please," came a little voice, and the baby kangaroo poked his head out of his mother's pouch. "Won't you show us?"

Somewhat disgruntled, the camel loped slowly into the middle of the circle of animals and started to dance. He swayed his hips and knocked his knees together; he twitched his ears and nodded his head. The band played along as best they could, but it was really the most peculiar dance they'd ever seen and it was impossible for them to keep time. The camel gave a funny sideways hop and waggled his humps from side to side, but this made him lose his balance, and he staggered across the grass and crashed into the musicians.

"Watch where you're putting your feet," scolded the squirrel, picking up his trampled pipe. But the camel hardly noticed. Even when the band stopped playing in protest, he kept on dancing. He kicked out his legs and hit a tree, bringing a family of bluebirds tumbling down. He swung his tail and knocked a row of rabbits flying, and then he backed into the giraffe and stood on the elephant's toes.

"Stop!" shouted the kangaroo. "For goodness' sake, stop!"

But the camel didn't stop. "I'm the best dancer," he panted. "See?" and he kept on flinging his clumsy feet all over the place. Soon, the animals were scrambling in all directions to get away from him.

It was only when the camel stomped on the lion's tail and was almost deafened by his ROAR of pain that he finally stopped. Looking around, he realized that his dance hadn't gone too well. The lion was glaring at him furiously, the mother kangaroo was shaking her head and the bushbaby was bawling her eyes out.

"Why isn't anyone clapping?" the camel asked crossly. "Didn't you like my dance?"

"Certainly not!" sniffed the llama.

"We liked you much better when you were giving us rides around the field," wailed the bushbaby.

"Or telling us stories of your desert adventures," added the bear cub.

"Oh," said the camel. He looked around at the broken musical instruments and the upset faces of all the animals. "I suppose it wasn't as much fun as the monkey's dance then?" he asked.

All the animals shook their heads.

The camel looked up at the monkey, who was dangling from a branch above his head. "You do dance extraordinarily well," he said awkwardly.

The monkey clambered down the tree and gave the camel a friendly pat on the humps. "And you, my friend, can walk for miles and miles without water, can tell a gripping desert tale or two, and seem to be extremely popular for giving rides on your humps," he said.

"Yes, dear," said the kangaroo in her motherly way. "Everyone's good at something different. Aren't they?"

The camel looked down at the tear-stained bushbaby. "There's no need to cry," he said gruffly. "If it would cheer you up, I suppose I could give you another ride."

"Yes, please!" beamed the bushbaby.

The camel lowered his long eyelashes with pride and pleasure. "Hop on then," he said.

The hare and the tortoise

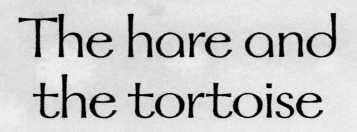

"Hurry up, slowcoach," teased the hare, bouncing up and down in front of the tortoise. "It's a wonder you ever get anywhere going that slowly."

"I get to where I need to go," replied the tortoise.

"And where's that?" mocked the hare. "About two inches away from where you started?"

"You leave him be," interrupted a small garden snail. "He's plenty fast enough."

"Maybe if you're used to going at a snail's pace," giggled the hare. "But if the tortoise and I had a race, you know very well who would win."

"You never know until you try," said the tortoise, with a wrinkly smile.

The hare missed a hop in amazement. "You can't seriously believe you'd be in with a chance?" he said, and even the snail looked a little surprised.

"I don't see why not," answered the tortoise solemnly.

"In that case," said the hare, "let's have a race. Tomorrow morning, at ten o'clock sharp, I'll race you from the top of the meadow to the barn at the bottom of the farmer's field."

"You're on," replied the tortoise.

"Goodness me," said the snail. "I have to see this," and she set out immediately, so as not to miss the finish.

Word about the race spread like wildfire. The snail told a fieldmouse, who whispered the news to a squirrel, who passed it on to a fox. A passing skylark overheard them and sang about it to anyone who would listen. By morning, animals from far and wide had come to watch the race.

At five to ten, the hare and the tortoise were limbering up on the starting line as the crowds lined up along the racetrack. The hare did twenty star-jumps and a dozen high springs to warm up. The tortoise simply stretched out his wrinkly legs one by one, and stared intently at the track before him.

"On your marks, please," called the pheasant, who had agreed to start the race. The hare and the tortoise crouched down, and a hush fell on the crowd. "Get set," said the pheasant. The onlookers craned forward. "GO!" shrieked the pheasant.

The hare shot off the starting line, bounding along at great speed. Within seconds, he was out of sight, zooming away in a cloud of dust. As the dust settled, the tortoise began to walk – very, *very* slowly – down the racetrack.

The crowd cheered and yelled encouragement at the tortoise. He was walking so slowly that many of them had shouted themselves hoarse by the time he actually passed them. But he kept on going at the same slow, steady pace.

Far ahead, the hare was speeding along, his long ears streaming out like banners behind him. Glancing over his shoulder, he realized that he'd left the tortoise a long way behind.

The hare was so confident of winning the race that he slowed down to wave at the clapping frogs and hollering foxes. He blew kisses to some leopard cubs and baby bears, and he even stopped to chat with a polar bear who had come all the way from the North Pole to see the race.

But soon, the hare had left the crowd a long way behind too. As the cheers died away, he could hear the humming of the bees and the twittering of the birds in the trees. It was a lovely, sunny day and before long the hare began to feel a little sleepy. "I've got plenty of time," he thought. "I may as well stop here for a short rest."

The hare hopped over to a tree beside the track and lay down in the dappled shade of its branches. "I'll just close my eyes," he murmured. "In a moment or two, I'll be as fresh as a daisy..." But in no time at all, the hare was fast asleep.

Meanwhile, the tortoise was still crawling along at the same slow pace. His supporters had started walking along the track beside him, taking turns to cheer him on. However, the tortoise was going so slowly that after a while their enthusiasm began to wane. They exchanged doubtful glances over the tortoise's back, and then a fox said what they had all been thinking – "The hare must have reached the finishing line by now."

But the tortoise paid no attention. With grim determination, he climbed the hill and began to make his way past the tree. "I don't believe it," smirked the fox when he saw the hare snoozing peacefully in the shade. "You may just be in with a chance, tortoise, old fellow." The tortoise's supporters let out a resounding cheer as he struggled over the top of the hill and began to make his way down the other side.

The cheers crept into the hare's slumber and he dreamed they were the roar of the crowd as he crossed the finishing line. His whiskers twitched with pride as he accepted an enormous golden trophy from a cheetah, who declared him to be the fastest runner in all the world.

By now, the tortoise had the finishing line in his sights. He kept plodding steadily along, without looking back over his shoulder or even glancing at his supporters, who were going wild with excitement. The little snail could hardly contain herself. "Come on, tortoise," she yelled, bobbing up and down on the finishing line. "You can do it!"

As the tortoise drew closer to the finishing line, the roar of the crowd got louder and louder, and the sleeping hare's ears pricked up a little as he slept. In his dream, the golden trophy had disappeared into thin air and the cheetah was roaring at him to hurry up.

Suddenly, the hare woke up with a jolt. "Where's my trophy?" he muttered, squinting in the bright sunshine. And then he realized. "Oh no!" he gasped. "I haven't crossed the finishing line yet!"

He scrambled to his feet and peered down the track. In the distance, he could just see the tortoise nearing the line. "No!" he wailed, haring down the hill. In his panic, he ran faster than he'd ever run in his life.

"Good heavens," remarked the fox in an amused voice. "Whatever is that?"

All the animals stared in astonishment. Racing towards them, barely visible in a blur of speed, was the hare. He was gaining on the tortoise at the most amazing rate. The crowd held their breath as he shot down the track like a rocket.

"Hurry up, tortoise," screamed the little snail. "Hurry UP!" But the tortoise kept on walking at the same, agonizingly slow pace.

"I can't let a tortoise beat me," thought the hare. "I have to win." For the final stretch, he ran like the wind. As he approached the finishing line, all he could hear was his blood thumping in his ears. Only a few more paces and victory would be his. The tortoise was just raising his foot to take the winning step. In desperation, the hare threw himself at the finishing line.

But it was too late. The tortoise, going so slowly he could have been in slow motion, stepped through the rope. A great roar broke out, and the crowd hoisted him onto their backs amid thunderous applause. The tortoise's face creased into a wide, triumphant smile.

The hare, meanwhile, sailed through the air and landed in the dust with a thud. "I'll never live this down," he groaned, covering his face with his paws.

"You see," piped a small voice. It was the garden snail, looking so proud she was almost ready to pop. "Slow and steady wins the race!"

The busy ant and the singing grasshopper

"Why don't you stop and enjoy the sun?" the grasshopper called to the ant as she hurried past.

The ant put down the large seed she was carrying and sighed. "I have too much to do," she said. "If I don't gather food for our store, my family won't have anything to eat in the winter."

"Who cares about winter?" replied the grasshopper drowsily. "You should enjoy the summer while it lasts." Closing his eyes, he began to sing a lazy summer song. He sang of the butterflies fluttering by; he sang of the flowers' sweet perfume; and he sang of long, summer days that seemed as though they would last forever.

The next day, the day after, and the one after that, the ant worked hard while the grasshopper did nothing but sunbathe and sing. Every time the ant passed by, the grasshopper invited her to stop for a while. But every time, the ant answered, "I can't stop now. I'm far too busy."

One day, when the summer was nearly over, the grasshopper said to the ant, "You must have enough in your store by now. You've been slaving away all summer."

"Have you any idea how big my family is?" the ant replied briskly. "Besides, don't you think you ought to be putting something away for yourself? I've heard it's going to be a cold winter. You'll need more than a song to keep you warm." And with that, she hurried on her way.

The grasshopper paid no attention. "Who wants to waste their life making preparations?" he said carelessly, and settled down under a dandelion to sing himself to sleep.

But, as the days went by, the sun began to lose its warmth. The butterflies disappeared and the leaves on the trees turned red and gold. Still, the grasshopper did nothing but sing. A chill crept in from the north, making him shiver. Men came to harvest their crops and before long the grasshopper found himself alone in an empty field, listening to the wind whistle through the stubbly stalks and howl across the sky.

He was cold and hungry, and he didn't feel much like singing any more. Thinking of all the food the ant had put away, the grasshopper decided to ask her for help.

He hopped along the ant's well-worn path and found her little doorway in the soil. "Little ant! Little ant!" he called. "Are you at home?"

The ant scurried to answer the door. All her tiny daughters and sons and nieces and nephews came too. They crowded into the doorway, curious to see who their visitor was.

"My! You really do have a big family!" exclaimed the grasshopper. "I was wondering," he continued hopefully, "whether you could spare me a morsel from your store. I'm cold and hungry now that winter has arrived."

"But what happened to your own store?" asked one of the tiny ants.

"Was it washed away in a terrible flood?" shrilled another.

"Or stolen by a big, scary bird?" suggested a third.

"Not exactly," said the grasshopper awkwardly. "I mean to say – I didn't actually make a store."

"But what were you doing all summer?" asked the tiniest ant of all.

The grasshopper blushed. "Not much," he said. "In fact…" he mumbled, looking down at his feet, "I wasn't really doing anything at all."

All of the tiny ants gasped in shock.

The mother ant frowned. "So now you expect to come and live off my store, do you? I worked hard all summer long to make my store, grasshopper," she said firmly, "and I have over a thousand mouths to feed."

"Oh dear," sighed the grasshopper. "Perhaps I should have prepared for the future a little after all, instead of just sunbathing and singing all summer." He turned to leave.

"Wait a moment," a tiny ant piped up. "Did you say you could sing?"

The grasshopper looked back and nodded. "That's right," he said. "That's one thing I *can* do."

"Oh, sing us a song!" cried the tiny ant.

"Perhaps he can sing for his supper," suggested another. "Can he, Mama? Can he?"

"Please let him," begged all the other tiny ants.

The mother ant folded her arms and looked sternly at the grasshopper. "Very well," she said. "Just this once."

And so all the ants settled down to listen to the grasshopper sing. It was a beautiful and haunting song. He sang of sunny days and butterflies; he sang of falling leaves and the howling wind; and he sang of the wisdom of ants, who work all summer long so they have something to put in their bellies when the cold winter sets in.

The trapped tiger

A man was walking through the woods one afternoon when he came across a tiger trapped in a cage. "Excuse me," called the tiger. "Would you be so kind as to let me out?"

The man took one look at the tiger's rippling muscles and dagger-like claws and said, "Do you think I'm some kind of fool? If I let you out, you'll just eat me up."

"Come on now – I wouldn't eat you," coaxed the tiger. "If you set me free, I'll be in your debt forever."

The man looked doubtful.

"Oh please," sobbed the tiger. "I'm begging you."

At the sight of a full-grown tiger crying like a baby, the man gave in. "All right, all right," he said. "I'll let you out. But remember what you said about not eating me."

He opened the door of the cage and out sprang the tiger. "Thank you very much," it snarled, and a slow, dangerous smile spread across its face. "Now I'm going to have you for my lunch."

"But – but that's not fair," stammered the man. "You just said that you wouldn't eat me."

The tiger threw back its head and laughed. "Fair?" it growled. "Who said anything about fair?"

It narrowed its amber eyes and stared at the man. Then it said, "I'll tell you what. In return for letting me out of the cage, I'll let you choose three judges. You can ask them whether it's fair for me to eat you. If they say it's unfair, I'll leave you alone. But if they think it's fair enough, you'll have to let me eat you up."

"Very well," agreed the man nervously. He looked around for somebody to ask, but there was no one in sight. So he walked up to the nearest tree and cleared his throat. "A tiger was trapped and I set it free. Is it fair if it eats me?" he asked.

The tree rustled its leaves. "Fair?" it whispered. "Is it fair that I offer men cool shade from the sun and, in return, they rip off my branches to feed to their cattle? Your fate is as fair as mine. What will be will be."

The man gulped as the tiger sharpened its claws. He hurried on through the woods. After a little way, he came across a buffalo turning a wheel at a well. "A tiger was trapped and I set it free. Is it fair if it eats me?" he asked.

"Ha!" snorted the buffalo. "Is it fair that all my life I've given people my milk to drink and now that I'm old they make me walk round and round all day in the hot sun? Your fate is as fair as mine. Face it like a man!"

The tiger's belly rumbled loudly. In desperation, the man fell to his knees and asked the road. "A tiger was trapped and I set it free. Is it fair if it eats me?" he said.

"Fair?" rasped the road, its voice a little dusty from lack of use. "Do you think it's fair that I show men the right way to go and just get trampled all over in return for my trouble? Your fate is as fair as mine. There's no way around it."

The tiger licked its lips in glee. "I think that just about settles it," it said. "Lie down here and prepare to be eaten."

Just then, a jackal came trotting by, whistling cheerfully. When it saw the tiger and the man, it stopped. "Hello," it said. "What's going on here?"

The man took a deep breath and told the jackal the whole story. When he'd finished, the jackal scratched its head. "How terribly confusing," it said. "Would you mind explaining it again?"

So the man explained all over again, while the tiger prowled around him, its tail twitching impatiently.

But the jackal still seemed totally confused. "You mean to say that you were in the cage and then the tiger came along – No, that's not quite right," it babbled. "You were in the tiger and then the cage came along – No. What was it again? The cage was in the tiger—"

"Fool!" snapped the tiger. "I was in the cage and this man came along and let me out."

"I see," beamed the jackal. "I was in the cage – oh, but I wasn't anywhere near it. Oh dear, oh dear. You'd better go ahead with your lunch. I don't think I'm ever going to understand."

"Oh yes you are," snarled the tiger, infuriated by the jackal's stupidity. "Listen carefully. I'm the tiger, right?"

"Right," nodded the jackal.

"And I was in this cage, right?"

"Right," agreed the jackal. "Well, no, actually," it said, shaking its head and frowning.

"What's the matter now?" roared the tiger, almost bursting with rage.

"Well, if you don't mind me asking," said the jackal, "how did you get into the cage in the first place?"

"Through the door, of course," growled the tiger.

"How do you mean?" asked the jackal.

By this point, the tiger had completely lost its patience. It leaped into the cage. "Like this!" it roared. "NOW do you understand?"

"Oh yes, perfectly," grinned the jackal, and slammed the cage door shut. "And I think perhaps it's best if we leave it at that!"

The clever little hare

"Stop that! Watch where you're going!" cried the little hare as an enormous elephant stepped on her tiny home, squashing it flat. But the elephant paid no attention.

Ever since they arrived at the lake, the elephants had been making the hares' lives a misery. It wasn't that the hares minded sharing the water — it had been a very dry summer and this was the only lake in the area that hadn't dried out. But as the elephants stomped around with their huge, clumsy feet, they squashed the hares' homes, frightened their children and

made their ears ache with all the endless trumpeting.

The hares had tried everything to make the elephants stop, but now even the oldest, wisest hare had run out of ideas. "Elephants take about as much notice of us as they do of the ants. There's simply nothing we can do," he shrugged.

"Nothing we can do?" muttered the little hare furiously as she rebuilt her home for the fifth time that week. "I'll see about that!"

That very night, as she gazed at the moon's reflection shimmering on the surface of the lake, the little hare came up with a plan.

The next evening, the little hare marched over to the largest, clumsiest elephant, who seemed to be the leader of the herd, and cleared her throat importantly.

The elephant leader swung his great head around, first looking left and then looking right. He didn't notice the little hare standing right by his toes.

"Hey!" shouted the little hare, scrambling up onto a large rock. "I'm HERE!"

The elephant peered at her. "Oh!" he trumpeted in surprise. His voice was so loud, that it almost blew the hare right off the rock. "Who are you?"

"I am a messenger," the little hare said, sitting up very straight and trying to look official. "I have been sent by Lord Moon to speak with you."

"I'm listening," boomed the elephant.

So the hare continued. "This lake belongs to Lord Moon, and the hares who live here have been specially appointed by him to guard it. You've been giving us all kinds of trouble with your thoughtless ways and your clumsy feet, and Lord Moon is very, very angry."

"I didn't know the lake belonged to Lord Moon," said the elephant doubtfully. "In fact, I've never heard of him."

"You've never heard of Lord Moon?" The hare staggered backwards, looking shocked. "Well, you can see him in the lake, as plain as the trunk on your face. Take a look."

The elephant looked and, sure enough, there in the middle of the lake, shimmering majestically on the surface of the water, was the moon. The huge animal gasped in awe.

Bending close to the elephant's ear, the hare whispered, "Be careful. He's really angry. But if you bow down to him and apologize, he might forgive you."

"Bow?" said the elephant. He shook his head slowly. "Elephants don't bow."

"Oh," said the hare. "Well, don't mind me. I'm only a messenger. I only suggested it because Lord Moon is so angry, and when he gets angry..." She shrugged and turned away. "I just wouldn't like to see you get hurt, that's all."

"Wait!" cried the elephant, and he pointed at the lake with his trunk. "Look at Lord Moon. What's he doing?" A gentle breeze had started to blow, rippling the surface of the lake and making the moon's reflection tremble.

"He's shaking with rage," whispered the hare. "Bow! Bow quickly! Apologize before it's too late."

To the hare's delight, the elephant bowed down low to the moon's reflection. "Lord Moon," he said, "please accept my deepest apologies for the trouble we've caused."

Just then, the breeze blew a little harder, making the moon's reflection quiver even more. "Oh dear," said the hare. "Look! You've made him even more angry."

"Oh no," the elephant moaned fearfully. "What can I do? Please help me."

"Let me try," said the hare. She bowed down so low that her ears touched the ground in front of her. "Lord Moon, please forgive the elephants," she said. "They are truly sorry and they promise never to come here again."

The breeze dropped, leaving the moon's reflection still and calm on the surface of the lake. The elephant heaved an enormous sigh of relief. "Thank you, little hare. Thank you!" he said gratefully.

After bowing once more to the moon's reflection, the elephant gathered his herd and left. All the elephants crept away on tiptoe, so they wouldn't disturb Lord Moon's hares, who were just settling down to sleep.

The town mouse and the country mouse

"Lunch in the countryside – how divine!" exclaimed the town mouse. An invitation from his cousin had arrived by bird-post just moments before. "Fresh air, sunshine, peace and quiet..." the little mouse continued dreamily, as he stared out of the window at the busy street below. "I bet food tastes delicious when you're lazing in a meadow under the open sky."

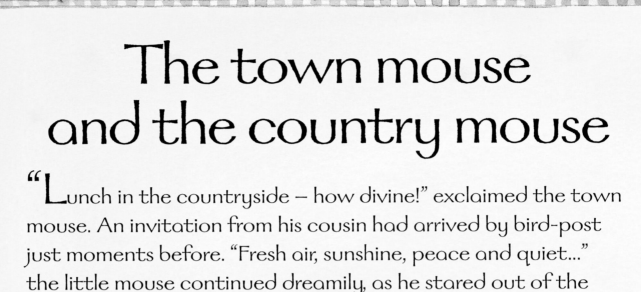

"Excuse me," said the postbird, who was waiting impatiently on the window ledge. "Will there be a reply?"

"Oh, yes, of course," said the mouse. "Please tell him I'd be delighted to come. I'll be there by noon tomorrow." The postbird nodded and swooped away into the sky.

Early the next morning, the little mouse slipped under the door of the town house where he lived, and set off to visit his cousin in the countryside.

He scurried along the busy streets, dodging through hurrying feet and dashing through the roaring traffic, until he reached the train station. Hundreds of passengers were piling off a train onto the platform, clutching briefcases and umbrellas. The little mouse slipped nimbly through their legs and hopped onto the train just in time. The doors closed behind him and the train pulled out of the station.

Clambering onto an empty window seat, the town mouse watched as the busy town flew by. Houses and shops, alleys and streets, people and lampposts, buses and cars whizzed past. Gradually, they gave way to rolling green hills and wide, flowery meadows.

When the train eventually stopped at a sleepy country station, the mouse hopped off. He skipped down the station steps and found himself in a quiet country lane. The air hummed gently with bees, and the sky burned bright, silent blue. There wasn't a rushing crowd or a roaring bus anywhere to be seen.

The little mouse pulled the invitation out of his bag to look at the directions his cousin had sent him. "Take the lane downhill from the station. Then turn left into the field," he read, "and keep going until you can hear the river. Turn right after the third daisy and you'll find my door underneath the poppies."

In no time at all, the town mouse was knocking on his cousin's little wooden door under the shade of the nodding poppies. His cousin flung open the door, squeaking with delight. "How lovely to see you!" he cried. "Do come in!"

The town mouse ducked his head and went inside. Like any country mouse's home, it was nothing more than a little hollow in the ground, with bare walls and a mud floor. But to the town mouse, used to grand houses with wallpapered walls and gleaming floors, it looked very dismal indeed. He didn't want to seem impolite, however, so he simply said, "Why don't we eat outside? It's such a glorious day!"

"Good idea," said the country mouse, and he scampered off to his storeroom to get their lunch. He bustled outside a moment later, carrying an armful of sunflower seeds. "Do help yourself," he said, as he laid them out on the grass.

The town mouse nibbled on a seed. "This is rather plain food," he thought. "Perhaps the next course will be a little more exciting."

The country mouse noticed his cousin wasn't eating very much. "Here," he said, offering him another sunflower seed, "do eat your fill."

"I don't want to fill up on the starter," smiled the town mouse. "I was saving my appetite for the main course."

"Main course?" said the country mouse in surprise. "But this is all there is."

The town mouse was astounded. "This is IT?" he squeaked. "But what do you live on the rest of the time?"

"More seeds," said the country mouse. "Occasionally, there's a strawberry or two, when they're in season..." He tailed off when he saw his cousin's horrified expression.

"No pies?" asked the town mouse. "No sandwiches or muffins or pieces of cheese?"

The country mouse shook his head.

"No chocolate cake or jam tart or ice cream?"

"I've never even tasted them," replied the country mouse.

"My dear cousin," said the town mouse, "you haven't *lived* until you've tasted ice cream." He stood up and pulled the country mouse to his feet.

"We have to leave right away," he said firmly. "You're coming to my house for dinner."

"But I've never gone beyond the edge of the field before," the country mouse panted as they scurried to the station.

"Then it's high time you did," answered the town mouse. They hopped onto the train and scrambled onto a window seat. As the train chugged through the countryside, the country mouse stared excitedly out of the window, his nose pressed right up against the glass. The fields gave way to houses and streets, buses and cars, and before long they found themselves in the busy town.

When they stepped out of the station, the country mouse's mouth dropped open. He quaked with terror at the cars that zoomed past, and trembled as an enormous bus screeched to a halt beside them. But the town mouse hardly seemed to notice. "Come on," he said, and dived into the traffic.

By the time they reached the house where the town mouse lived, his country cousin had almost been stepped on, very nearly run over and was utterly exhausted.

154

"Welcome to my humble home," said the town mouse, and the two mice slipped under the front door.

The country mouse gasped. There were gleaming tiles as far as he could see, walls covered in strange and beautiful flowers, and a crystal chandelier that shone like the sun.

"Are you hungry?" asked the town mouse.

"Ravenous," said the country mouse.

"Well what are we waiting for?" laughed his cousin. The pair scampered across the tiles into the dining room and ran up the leg of the enormous dining table.

"Dinner is served," said the town mouse grandly.

The country mouse's mouth dropped open in amazement. He'd never seen so much wonderful food in all his life. There were mountains of cheese and rows of crumbling biscuits, great bunches of purple grapes and stacks of mouthwatering sandwiches, and, at the far end of the table, more cakes and delicious desserts than he'd ever dreamed of.

"Help yourself," said the town mouse, his cheeks already bulging with cheese.

The country mouse wandered around the table in a daze, plucking a grape here and nibbling on a sandwich there. He climbed all over the cheeses, tasting a mouthful of each different kind.

"Wheee!" his cousin shrieked from across the table, and he slid down a spoon into a bowl of whipped cream.

"Wait for me!" the country mouse shouted gleefully and he ran to join in the fun.

By the time he had stuffed his mouth full of chocolate cake, licked all the frosting off a cherry slice and munched his way stickily through a large strawberry tart, the country mouse decided he felt entirely at home in the town. He was just wiping his paws on a crisp, white napkin when the town mouse called, "Come with me.

I've got a surprise for you." Taking his cousin by the paw, he led him over to a cold glass bowl with huge pink and white balls in it. "This..." said the town mouse dramatically, "is ice cream."

They swung themselves up on a spoon and jumped into the bowl. "It's freezing cold!" exclaimed the country mouse.

"Of course it is," said the town mouse. "Try it."

His cousin dipped a paw into the ice cream and licked it. It sent sweet, icy shivers of delight down the little mouse's spine. "It's heaven!" he sighed, closing his eyes in bliss.

Suddenly, the dining room door flew open and a man walked into the room. As quick as a flash, the town mouse jumped down and hid behind the ice cream bowl. But the country mouse was glued to the spot with fright. "Hide!" whispered the town mouse. "Quickly, before he sees you."

Coming to his senses, the country mouse dived between two scoops of ice cream. It was colder than the middle of winter, but he didn't dare move. He crouched down, shivering, until he heard the sound of the door closing again and saw his cousin's face looking down at him.

"Is-s it s-s-afe t-to c-c-ome out now?" said the country mouse, his teeth chattering with cold.

"Yes," said the town mouse, pulling his cousin out of the bowl and brushing the frost off his whiskers. "Come and eat some apple pie," he said reassuringly. "That will warm you up."

They were just heading for the steaming apple pie at the end of the table when there was a loud "MEOW".

"Uh-oh," said the town mouse.

Before the country mouse could even ask what the matter was, a gigantic, ferocious-looking cat sprang up onto the table right in front of them.

"Run for your life!" shrilled the town mouse.

This time, his cousin didn't hesitate. The pair fled helter-skelter down the table, with the cat hot on their tails. They shot past the chocolate cake, slipped between two plates and raced around the cheeseboard.

Hissing ferociously, the cat bounded after them, knocking glasses over and sending bowls flying in every direction.

The mice reached the edge of the table just in time. As the country mouse leaped off the table, he felt the cat's claws swish past his back. He landed on the soft carpet, his heart pounding in panic. Behind him, the cat spat with fury as it skidded to the edge of the table, clawing at the tablecloth to try to keep its balance.

"Over here!" squeaked the town mouse, pointing towards a little hole in the skirting board, and the two mice raced across the carpet.

There was a yowl and an almighty crash as the cat fell to the floor, pulling the tablecloth and all the plates and glasses down after it. Without stopping to look back, the two little mice dived into the hole and collapsed in a heap, their sides heaving. "That's just a little drawback of living the high life," panted the town mouse.

"You call that a *little* drawback?" gasped his cousin. "Well, as far as I'm concerned, you can keep your high life. I'm off back to the countryside just as soon as I've caught my breath."

"What?" said the town mouse. "And live without all this heavenly food?"

"Yes," said the country mouse.

"Even ice cream?" added the town mouse.

"Even ice cream," said the country mouse firmly. "I'd rather have my peace and quiet than risk life and limb for a pawful of ice cream."

Legends
of
monsters
and
dragons

George and the dragon

"Enough is enough," declared the king. "It's time to fight back." The crowd cheered and charged down to the lake. But, a few moments later, they came charging back with a ferocious dragon hot on their heels. "Close the gate," they yelled, tumbling into the town.

They were just in time. As the gate slammed shut, the dragon crashed against it. It was hungry and very, very angry. "Send out the sheep!" shouted the king. The guards opened the gate just a little and pushed out two frightened sheep.

The dragon snatched them up one after the other. With two loud gulps, it swallowed them whole, and then thundered away down the hill.

Everyone breathed a huge sigh of relief, except the king's chief advisor, who was looking rather worried. "Ahem," he coughed nervously. "I'm afraid that was the last of the sheep."

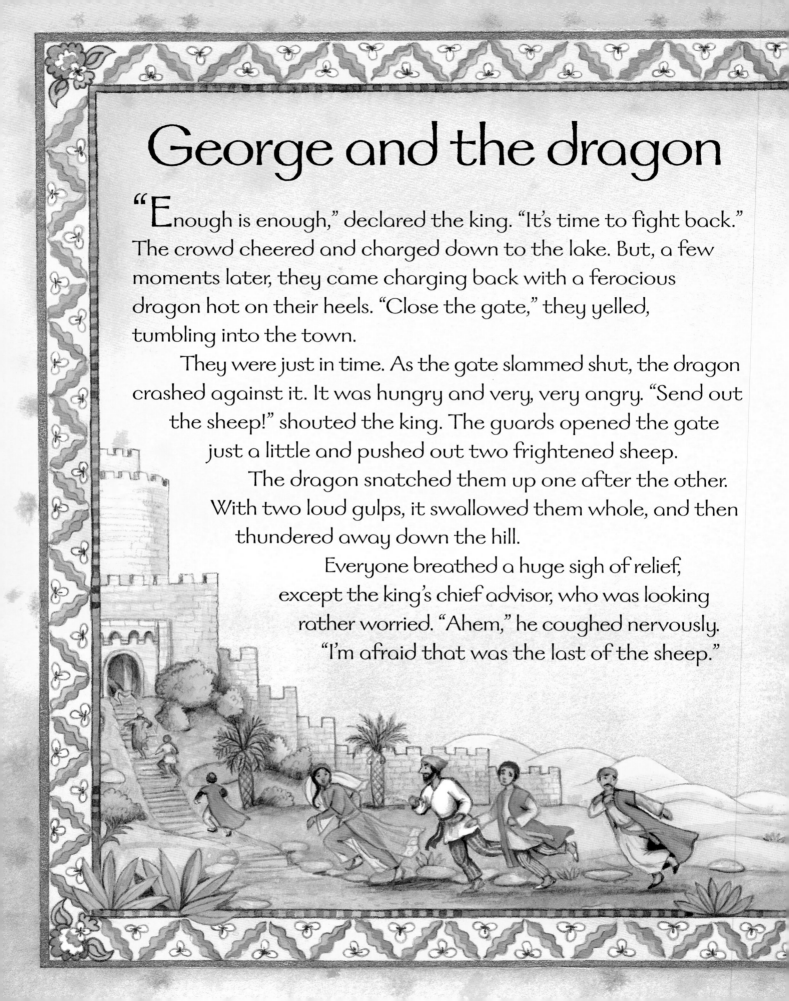

There was a silence. "You all know what that means," said the king sadly. "There's nothing left for the dragon to eat. Tomorrow, everyone's names will be put into a pot, and the person whose name is pulled out must be fed to the dragon."

The very next day that was just what happened, and the day after, and the day after that. As long as the dragon had enough to eat, it left the rest of them alone.

Then, one day, the princess's name was pulled out of the pot. The king turned pale. "Not my lovely daughter," he begged. "Take all my gold and silver and even my entire kingdom, but please don't take my daughter."

His people were furious. "This was your idea," they shouted. "We've given up our children to feed that monster. Why should you be any different?"

The king was heartbroken, but he knew they were right. "Forgive me," he said, throwing his arms around the princess.

Eventually, the king tore himself away, and collapsed on the ground, weeping. His people wept with him, for in spite of their anger they all loved the princess too.

The princess walked slowly through the crowd and made her way to the lake where the dragon lived. There, she sat down all alone and waited, with tears trickling down her face.

After a little while, she heard the sound of hooves, and a handsome knight rode up to her. "What's wrong?" he asked. "Is there something I can do to help?"

"If you want to help yourself, you'd better leave now," sobbed the princess.

The knight didn't move. "My name is George," he said gently, "and I'm not going anywhere until you tell me why you're crying."

So the princess began to tell him all about the dragon. But, before she had finished, she was interrupted by a terrible roar. The dragon reared up out of the lake and ran at them, its eyes blazing.

George lowered his lance and charged. When the lance struck the dragon's chest, it splintered into a thousand tiny pieces, for the dragon's heart was harder than any stone.

As the dragon spun around in fury, its whip-like tail knocked George off his horse. Quickly, he sprang to his feet and drew his sword. With all of his strength, he lunged at the dragon, but it hardly even seemed to notice.

The dragon spread out its wings and took to the air.
It circled three times, then swooped down, shooting flames
from its mouth. It was almost upon them when George saw
his chance. Beneath its wings was soft, pale flesh. Quickly,
he thrust his sword upwards. The dragon let out a deafening
shriek and tumbled to the ground.

George rushed over to it. It was lying very still, but it
was alive. He turned to the princess. "Give me your sash,"
he said. "Let's take the dragon back with us, so everyone can
see that it won't hurt them any more."

George tied the sash around the dragon's neck and tugged
on it gently. With a groan, the beast lumbered to its feet. The
princess gasped and shrank back, but the dragon hung its head
meekly, and she saw to her surprise that it was no longer a threat.

Together, George and the princess led the dragon into
the town. Everyone screamed and ran inside. "Don't worry,"
called George. "We've tamed it. Come and see."

A few people peered around their doors. "He's right!"
exclaimed one man. "It's like a pet dog."

"Whoever would have thought it?" said the man's wife, shaking her head.

Soon, the whole town was out in the streets, clapping and cheering. The king heard the noise and came to see what was happening. "Oh, happiest of days," he cried when he saw the princess. Sweeping her up in his arms, he hugged her until she could hardly breathe.

At last, he turned to George. "Brave knight," he said, "you have saved us all. Please, name your reward."

"Thank you," replied George. "Please don't think me rude, but I already have all that I need. I must leave now — there are others who need my help." And a moment later he was gone.

But the dragon stayed on in the town, living in the castle gardens. From then on, the only people who were afraid of it were the king's enemies, so it made the perfect guard-dragon.

Odysseus and the Cyclops

After many months at sea and all kinds of strange adventures, Odysseus and his men came to an island. They were running low on supplies, so they landed there to stock up.

Odysseus filled a goatskin bottle with wine and he and a few companions set out to explore. After a while, Odysseus spotted a cave high up in the cliffs. "Let's see what's up there," he said to his men.

It was a steep climb and by the time they reached the cave everyone was exhausted.

"Is there anybody there?" Odysseus called. There was no reply, so he stepped inside to look around. At the front, he found some enormous bowls of milk and large baskets of cheese. "We've struck lucky here," he called to the others. "Come inside and let's eat."

They were all munching away when they heard heavy footsteps outside. Suddenly, the cave went dark. Standing in the entrance, blocking out the sun, was a Cyclops, a huge giant with a single, staring eye right in the middle of its forehead.

Odysseus and his men dived behind the rocks at the back of the cave, their hearts thumping. Slowly, the Cyclops looked around the cave. To their relief, it didn't see them.

They watched as the Cyclops herded a flock of sheep into the cave. When all the sheep were inside, it rolled a massive rock across the entrance to close it like a door. As the Cyclops turned around, it caught sight of them crouching behind the rocks. "Who are you?" it boomed, "and what are you doing in my cave?"

Terror seized their hearts. Only Odysseus was brave enough to speak. "We are Greek soldiers on our way home from Troy," he said. "We have lost our way and landed here in search of food and water..."

Before Odysseus could finish, the Cyclops grabbed two of his men in its enormous fist and stuffed them into its mouth. Odysseus stared in horror, but there was absolutely nothing he could do.

The Cyclops paid no more attention to the rest of the men. Instead, it lay down on the floor of the cave. A few minutes later it was sleeping soundly.

"We must kill that thing or it will eat us all," whispered one of the men.

"No," replied Odysseus. "If we kill it, we'll be trapped here for good. We'd never be able to push that rock away from the entrance. Let's be patient."

It was a long night in the dark cave and only a crack of light around the entrance told them when morning had finally arrived. At last, the Cyclops woke up. It rolled away the rock and herded the sheep out of the cave. Then, before Odysseus and his men could slip out, it heaved the rock back into place.

169

The men exchanged looks of
despair. "Don't worry," said Odysseus.
"I've got a plan." He picked up a piece of
wood and cut it into a point to make a spear.
Then he hid it at the back of the cave, and they
all settled down to wait for the Cyclops to return.
Eventually, they heard heavy footsteps,
followed by a grating sound as the Cyclops shoved
the rock aside. It herded in the sheep just as it had the
night before and pushed the rock back again.

The Cyclops was just beginning to light a fire
when Odysseus stepped forward. "Would you like
some wine?" he said. Without waiting for an
answer, he poured some wine into a bowl
and offered it to the Cyclops.

Behind the rocks, his men held their
breath in anticipation. The Cyclops took
the bowl and, with a flick of its head, it
knocked the wine back in a single gulp.

Odysseus filled the bowl again. "What's your name?" asked the Cyclops, swigging the wine down.

"I'm called Nobody," said Odysseus, emptying the rest of the wine into the bowl.

The Cyclops took the bowl from him and finished it off. "That's a strange name," it yawned. Its head began to nod and soon the Cyclops was snoring loudly.

"Now's our chance," whispered Odysseus. He picked up the spear he'd made and thrust it into the fire. When it was burning hot, he crept up to the sleeping Cyclops and plunged it into the giant's huge eye with all his might.

The Cyclops let out a bellow of pain. Leaping to its feet, it stumbled around the cave, clutching its eye.

Some Cyclopses living in the nearby caves heard the noise and hurried to see what was wrong. "What's happening in there?" they called.

"Nobody has hurt me," cried the Cyclops.
"Well, if nobody has hurt you, what are you making such a fuss about?" they demanded.

"Nobody has blinded me," wailed the Cyclops in despair.

"What nonsense you talk! Stop wasting our time," grumbled the others, and they went back to their caves.

Odysseus was delighted with how well his plan had worked, but it wasn't over yet. They still had to get away. Working quickly and quietly, he caught the sheep and tied them together in threes.

When he had finished, Odysseus turned to his men. "Listen carefully," he whispered. "Here's how we'll make our escape. When the Cyclops lets the sheep out to graze, you must cling on under the bellies of the middle ones."

In the morning, the Cyclops pushed back the rock once more. As the sheep trotted up to the Cyclops, Odysseus's men held on tightly. The Cyclops stroked the sheep's backs to check that no one was trying to sneak out with them. But it didn't feel the men clinging on underneath, so it allowed them to pass.

As soon as all the men were safely outside, Odysseus yelled, "Run for the ship." They raced down to the shore, seized the oars and rowed away as fast as they possibly could.

When the Cyclops realized they had gone, he staggered blindly to the clifftops and hurled huge rocks after them. The rocks crashed into the water, narrowly missing the ship. It was a good thing for Odysseus and his men that the Cyclops couldn't see.

They rowed on until the ship was out of reach. Then they let down the sail and the wind blew them on their way. At last, they were safe... although many more adventures still lay ahead.

The big fish

Once there was a poor fisherman. He had been fishing all day, but he hadn't caught a single thing. As the sun sank in the evening sky, he began to haul in his net one last time. To his surprise, it felt heavy. He peered hopefully over the edge of the boat to see what he had caught. There, beneath the waves, a huge shadowy shape was struggling in the net. "What a whopper!" he cried. "I'll have a feast tonight."

Forgetting his tiredness, the fisherman grabbed hold of the ropes and started to pull. He tugged and heaved, and heaved and tugged, until sweat poured down his face, but he couldn't pull the net up. He paused for a moment and took a deep breath. Then, gathering all the strength in his skinny body, he pulled and pulled with all his might. He pulled so hard that the little boat nearly capsized, but the net hardly seemed to move.

The fisherman slumped to his knees and put his head in his hands. "That one fish would be enough to feed everyone in my village for a whole month," he thought to himself. "I can't just let it go." But he realized that, no matter how hard he tried, he'd never be able to haul it in by himself.

"I've got it!" thought the fisherman suddenly. "If I can just get the fish back to the shore, there'll be plenty of people to help me." He tied the net to the back of his boat and, very slowly, he began to row home.

He hadn't gone far when he heard splashing behind him. Glancing back, he saw a flash of golden scales. The big fish was struggling in the net and churning up the water. Worried that his fine catch might escape, the fisherman tried to row faster.

A little later, the fisherman thought he heard a voice. He stopped rowing and listened, but all he could hear was the sound of the waves lapping against the boat. Yet as soon as he started to row, he thought he heard it again. "All this excitement must be getting to me," muttered the fisherman.

Then he heard it absolutely clearly: a rich, silvery voice that sounded as though it came from another world. "Please let me go," it said.

The fisherman looked over his shoulder nervously and his eyes almost popped out of his head. This was no fish; it was a monster! On top of its sleek, scaly body was the fearsome head of a dragon. With a squeal of fright, the fisherman threw himself down in the bottom of the boat and cowered there, trembling.

"Don't be afraid," said the creature softly. "I won't hurt you." Lifting his head doubtfully, the fisherman met its eyes. "I only want to be free," it said.

The fisherman weighed up the situation. It was certainly more than he had bargained for, but this beast didn't sound nearly as scary as it looked, and he was extremely hungry. "It is trapped in the net," he thought to himself. "What harm could it do?"

Feeling a little braver, the fisherman began to row again. Soon, the creature's voice rose above the lapping of the waves once more. "Have a heart," it begged. "I just want to go home."

The fisherman sighed. Somehow, he didn't think his dinner would taste quite the same any more. With a heavy heart and a rumbling tummy, he leaned over the side of the boat and cut the net.

Delighted to be free, the dragon-fish hurled itself into the air, its golden scales gleaming in the light of the setting sun. The fisherman gazed in awe as the majestic creature splashed into the sea.

When it rose to the surface again, the dragon-fish bowed its great head solemnly. "Thank you, my friend," it said. "I am the son of the Dragon King, who rules the sea. I will not forget your kindness."

The fisherman opened his mouth to speak, but before he could find any words the creature had disappeared beneath the waves. "There goes my feast," he sighed, and he began to row home.

The fisherman was still feeling sorry for himself when he went fishing the next morning, but as he caught more and more fish he began to cheer up.

The morning after that, the fisherman's boat had hardly left the shore before the net was full to bursting with fat, shiny fish.

On the third morning, he hadn't even lowered his net into the water when a wet fish landed at his feet. "What on Earth?" he exclaimed, as another fish slapped him in the face. It was incredible. The fish were leaping into the boat all by themselves.

The fisherman stared into the water in disbelief and, from fathoms below, in another world, he heard a familiar voice. "I haven't forgotten you," it said.

From that day on, the fisherman never had any trouble catching fish. And whenever he heard fishermen boasting about the size of the fish they had caught, he would just smile to himself and say nothing.

The Chimaera

"I've brought this from your son-in-law," said Prince Bellerophon, handing a letter to King Iobates.

"Never mind that," said the king warmly. "You've only just arrived. Come on in and make yourself at home."

Several days later, the king finally got around to opening the letter, and when he did he was horrified. It said that Bellerophon had insulted his daughter and appealed to him to have the prince killed.

King Iobates felt very uncomfortable about the idea of killing a guest, but he couldn't let him get away with insulting his daughter. He thought carefully and eventually he came up with a way to get rid of the prince without getting his own hands dirty.

He called Bellerophon to him. "I need your help," he said. "A terrible creature is killing my people. It's called the Chimaera. It has the head of a lion, the body of a goat and the tail of a snake. Many brave men have died fighting it, but I'm sure you could kill it." In fact, he felt sure the Chimaera would kill the prince.

The bold young prince accepted the challenge at once. Before setting out on his quest, he went to visit a wise old man named Polyidus to seek his advice. "How can I defeat this monster?" he asked.

"It is a dangerous task," Polyidus
told him. "To have any hope of killing the
Chimaera, you'll need to ride on Pegasus, the
winged horse, and attack it from above. But first
you must capture Pegasus. It won't be easy. I suggest
that you ask the goddess Athena for help."

That night, Bellerophon prayed to Athena and the
goddess appeared to him in a dream. "Take this," she said,
holding out a bridle. "It will help you to capture Pegasus."

When Bellerophon woke up, he was clutching the bridle
Athena had given him. Eagerly, he set off in search of Pegasus.
It was almost nightfall when he found him, drinking at a stream.
Very quietly, Bellerophon crept up on Pegasus, and when he was
close enough, he flung the bridle over the horse's head.

Pegasus snorted and reared up,
trying to escape. Bellerophon clung onto the bridle.
"Calm down," he said soothingly.

Pegasus gradually became quieter and Bellerophon was able to climb onto his back. As Bellerophon nudged him with his heels, Pegasus spread his wings and sprang into the air. Higher and higher they flew, over lakes and rivers, valleys and hills, searching for the Chimaera. Eventually, Bellerophon caught sight of it far below. He pulled gently on the bridle, and Pegasus swooped down.

The Chimaera was as strange and as terrifying as the king had said. Its mouth shot out red-hot flames and its snake-tail spat deadly poison.

As they flew closer, the Chimaera lashed out with its powerful front claws, threatening to snatch them from the sky. Pegasus pulled up sharply, almost sending Bellerophon plunging to the ground.

The prince steadied himself and they dived again. When they were close enough, he raised his bow and arrow and aimed at the Chimaera's head. He fired just as Pegasus swerved to dodge the flames shooting from the Chimaera's mouth, and the arrow went into its side.

He swung Pegasus around and they flew down again. "Steady now," urged Bellerophon. Again, he took aim. This time he waited for the beast to open its mouth, and then fired right into it. It stopped mid-roar and fell to the ground. The terrible monster was dead.

Bellerophon flew at once to King Iobates' palace to tell him the good news. When the king saw him riding on a winged horse, he could hardly believe his eyes, and when he heard how Bellerophon had defeated the Chimaera, he began to doubt his ears too. "He must be descended from the gods themselves," thought the king nervously.

The prince's fame spread across the land and everywhere he went people praised him for his bravery. The king even gave him half his kingdom as a reward, which was just as it should be, for the brave prince had never insulted the king's daughter in the first place.

The Minotaur

Beneath King Minos's palace was a vast maze called the Labyrinth – a network of tunnels so intricate that no one could ever find their way out. The king had it built when his wife gave birth to the Minotaur, a hideous monster with the body of a man and the head of a bull. This strange underground world became its home.

Every year, King Minos demanded that seven men and seven women were sent from Athens to be fed to the Minotaur. Once they entered the Labyrinth, they were never seen again.

It was that time of year now and the King of Athens faced the terrible task of choosing who to send. "Choose me," begged his son, Theseus. "I'll kill the Minotaur and no one else will have to die."

His father looked doubtful, but Theseus was brave and determined, and so eventually he agreed.

When the fourteen young Athenians were brought before King Minos, his daughter, Ariadne, could hardly take her eyes off Theseus. She waited until her father was out of earshot and pulled Theseus to one side. "No one survives the Labyrinth," she whispered. "Let me help you escape."

"I don't want to run away," said Theseus. "I've come here to kill the Minotaur."

Ariadne stared at him. His bright eyes were eager for adventure. "I can see you're not afraid," she said, "but you'll never succeed alone. If you promise to take me away with you, I'll help you." Theseus was a little taken aback, but he smiled and agreed.

Early the next morning, Ariadne led Theseus to the entrance of the Labyrinth. "Take this," she said, slipping a ball of silken thread into his hand. She tied the other end to the doorpost. "Let it unwind as you go," she added. "Without it, you'll never find your way out."

Theseus thanked her and strode bravely into the Labyrinth, letting out the thread as he went. He walked down dark, twisting tunnels and around many corners, further and further in. Each passage looked the same as the last, and Theseus began to despair of ever finding the Minotaur. Then, suddenly, he heard it.

The Minotaur's bellows echoed throughout the tunnels, making it sound more like a hundred monsters. Boldly, Theseus made his way to where he thought the sound was coming from.

He turned a corner and there it was ahead of him, its red eyes glowing fiercely in the darkness.

For what seemed like the longest moment of Theseus's life, the Minotaur stared at him. Then it lowered its head and charged. He stood his ground as it came closer and closer. Right at the last moment, he stepped lightly aside and it ran straight past him.

The Minotaur swung around, snorting in fury. Although it had the body of a man, there was nothing human about this creature. It charged again. Theseus waited until it was almost upon him, then he quickly drew his sword. It was too late for the Minotaur to swerve and it ran straight onto the blade. With a mournful bellow, it sank to the ground, dead.

Theseus looked back and saw the silken thread gleaming in the darkness, a lifeline to the world above. He caught hold of it and, winding it up as he went, hurried back through the twisting tunnels of the Labyrinth.

When he reached the entrance, Ariadne was waiting. Her face lit up as she saw him. "I've done it. I've killed the Minotaur," he gasped, "but we must hurry. Our work's not finished yet."

Theseus grabbed Ariadne's hand and they raced through the palace to where the Athenians were imprisoned. As quietly as he could, Theseus slid back the bolt. "Follow me and don't make a noise," he whispered to the young Athenians.

Together, they all ran back to the ship and leaped aboard. Seizing the oars, they rowed out to sea and hoisted the sail. The wind caught hold of it and they sped over the water on their way back to Athens.

Rustam's faithful horse

Prince Rustam had been riding all day and he was exhausted. As night fell, he settled down beneath a tree to rest, and before long he was sound asleep.

Rustam's horse, Rakush, was keeping watch nearby. The trees shuddered in the wind, making him restless. His keen ears twitched at every little sound. Suddenly, the wind changed. Rakush's nostrils quivered; he could smell danger in the night air.

A moment later, there was a flash of gold between the trees. In a single powerful leap, a lion sprang onto the horse's back. Screaming with terror, Rakush reared up on his hind legs. Somehow, he managed to fling the lion aside.

It turned around, snarling ferociously. Rakush reared up again, waving his front legs wildly in the air. With deadly force, he brought his hooves crashing down on the lion's head. The life faded from its eyes and it fell to the ground.

Rustam rushed over, his sword at the ready, but he saw immediately that the lion was already dead. "Brave, brave horse, you have saved both our lives," he said, patting Rakush's neck. "But please be careful, my friend. If anything like this happens again, you must wake me up."

The next day, they crossed a vast expanse of rocky desert. The sun's rays burned down upon them, and there was no shade or water anywhere.

Eventually, just as the sun was sinking down in the sky, they came to a spring. It was a welcome sight. Desperately thirsty, Rustam fell to his knees and began to scoop the cool, refreshing water into his mouth. When he had finished, he lay down beside the spring and fell fast asleep.

Rakush stepped forward to drink too, but as he lowered his head, he thought he heard a noise. He gave a snort of alarm.

Rustam jumped up. "What is it? Where?" he demanded, spinning around to face every direction in turn. There was nothing there. Rustam relaxed. "You silly horse," he said affectionately. "What are you panicking about? The lion's dead. Calm down and let's get some sleep."

Rustam lay down and soon he was snoring away, but Rakush couldn't settle. As the moon drifted in and out of the clouds, the horse peered anxiously into the darkness. Everything was still and silent. Then, suddenly, Rakush saw what had been making the noise. Out of the shadows loomed the unmistakable shape of a dragon. It came closer and closer. Rakush neighed loudly and beat the ground with his hooves. To his astonishment, the dragon vanished.

Rustam sat bolt upright. "What is it? What's going on?" he cried in confusion. Then he saw Rakush prancing nervously from side to side. "What's the matter now?" he groaned.

Rustam searched all around, but he couldn't find anything out of the ordinary.

"You see," he said to Rakush. "There's absolutely nothing to worry about. Now settle down."

Rakush shook his head.

"Look, I need some sleep," said Rustam wearily. "If you can't behave yourself, I'm afraid I'll have to tie you up." He slipped a rope around the horse's neck and tied it to a tree. "Now, don't wake me again," he said firmly.

No sooner was Rustam asleep than Rakush caught sight of the dragon's red eyes in the bushes. They scanned around greedily until they settled on his sleeping master. Rakush jerked at the rope, but it was tied tightly.

As the dragon came closer and closer, Rakush looked from Rustam to the dragon and back again, sweating with anguish. What should he do? In a few more seconds, his master would certainly be dead. He could bear it no longer. In desperation, he let out a shrill whinny.

Rustam almost jumped out of his skin. "What NOW?" he yelled, but the sight of the hideous dragon right before him silenced Rustam instantly. He rolled out of the way as the dragon lunged at his throat. Then, grabbing his sword and shield, he scrambled to his feet.

The dragon glared at Rustam in contempt. Then it opened its mouth and blasted the shield with its fiery breath. In a second, the shield was scorched to cinders.

Seeing the danger his master was in, Rakush reared up with all of his strength. The rope snapped and he leaped to Rustam's aid.

As the dragon turned to face its new enemy, Rustam darted forward, his sword raised. With deadly force, he brought the sword down, slicing right through the dragon's neck. Its head thudded to the ground, and then its body rolled slowly sideways.

Breathing heavily, Rustam turned to Rakush. "It's dead," he said, wiping the sweat from his brow. He reached out to stroke Rakush, but the horse shied away, remembering how his master had scolded him.

"I'm so sorry," said Rustam. "I shouldn't have doubted you. Can you ever forgive me?"

The horse gazed steadily back at his master with his large brown eyes. Then he lowered his head and nuzzled him.

Rustam smiled and stroked Rakush's velvety nose. "What would I do without you, my faithful friend?" he said.

With thanks to the following for advice about the stories:
Dr. Arshia Sattar, James Brown and Dr. Abigail Wheatley.

First published in 2006 by Usborne Publishing Ltd,
Usborne House, 83-85 Saffron Hill, London EC1N 8RT, England.
www.usborne.com Copyright © 2006 Usborne Publishing Ltd.
The name Usborne and the devices ♀ 🌐 are Trade Marks of Usborne Publishing Ltd.
First published in America in 2007. U.E. Printed in Dubai.